From
the Abyss *of*
Darkness

Other Books By Author

～

Rain

This heartwarming love story takes the reader through Valentina's journey from homeless to hopeful, proving the human spirit's resilience and ability to find kindness and love when, and where, least expected.

Dedication

To my incredible husband - XO

Acknowledgments

For the extraordinary loves in my life,
Dan, Sonia, Missy,
Mackenzie and Logan;
You inspire me to be the best version of
me. I love you; always and forever! XO

From
the Abyss *of*
Darkness

Marcelina
Nóbrega Courtney

Chapter 1

JAKE WOKE TO a relentless pounding, unsure if it was his head or someone at the door. He lifted his head and realized it was both.

He rolled over on the sofa where he'd spent the night and yanked a pillow over his head, drowning out the noise—or attempting to.

"Jake! I know you're in there. And I'm not leaving." More knocking followed his mother's threat.

Throwing the pillow onto the floor, he forced his uncooperative body into motion. Along with his headache, his mouth was sandbox dry and nausea churned his gut, though his stomach was empty.

Climbing to his feet, the darkness in the house left him disoriented, and he didn't know whether it was night or day, let alone which day of the week it might be. Honestly, he didn't care.

Jake's energy was gone since the accident, but he shuffled toward the front door. When he opened it, his mother forced her way in, casting a look of both disdain and profound love upon him.

He knew she despised the man he had become, a far cry from the healthy, happy figure he had been. He also knew what he looked like—unkempt hair, weeks-old clothing, yellowed teeth, and a repugnant odor told a story of his descent into despair.

Covering his eyes to shield them from the harsh light pouring in through the door, Jake waited for her to speak.

"Son, what are you doing with your life? We raised you better than this. I understand you're hurting but you have a family who loves you and wants to help." She brushed past him and laid her purse on the hall table. "Please. Your daughter loves you, needs you, and misses you. She asks about you all the time. Ivy misses her mom, but she's gone. Must she lose you too?" Her tone was pleading.

Tears streamed down Jake's face as he stood there, struggling to find words. He knew she was right. Ivy was all he had left of Emma, yet…

He shook his head, unable to explain, and longed to return to the numbness that alcohol provided.

He missed his daughter's sweet face, her innocence, her love, her hugs and kisses, but the loss was still too overwhelming for him to take care of her. Besides, Ivy's resemblance to her late mother, in her eyes, hair, smile, and laugh, only intensified his pain. Drinking had become his refuge to temporarily escape the agony, but what started as a temporary reprieve had turned into months of descent into a menacing abyss, and he knew his family was worried sick about him.

His mom held Jake in her arms, and they stood in silence for a few moments. Then she looked up at him. "I love you, son. I know that won't ease your pain, but your father and I are here for you. If you want to cry, do it. If you want to scream, let it out. If you want to talk, I'm here to listen. Talking is a good start, but you can't keep disconnecting from the world. Eventually, you have to face it. If you keep going like this, Ivy will lose you too."

He knew that. But denial of what happened had turned into depression, which had morphed into seething anger, intensified by his heavy reliance on alcohol. Acceptance, it seemed, was a distant goal that he wasn't sure he'd ever achicvc.

Amelia planted a tender kiss on her son's cheek before stepping away. She flicked the lights on, unveiling the neglect and disarray of the house. Dust obscured furniture and moldings, clothes had melded with the floor, and empty bottles of beer and hard liquor littered the entire space. Take-out containers once holding food, now sat with remnants of either dry or sickeningly green and radiated unpleasant odors.

She shook her head but held her tongue. Then, armed with a large garbage bag, she started cleaning.

"Go wash up. Once I'm done here I'm going to make something to eat and you're going to eat it."

Jake nodded, knowing he needed both a shower and food. But what he *wanted* was another drink.

AFTER HE SHOWERED, shaved, and put on clean, albeit wrinkled clothes, he looked markedly better, although still a shadow of his former self. Pain etched across his face, replacing the constant smile he once wore.

In the kitchen, he reached for a beer, but Amelia replaced it with a cup of black coffee and a plate of scrambled eggs.

He mumbled a begrudging thanks and sat at the table, trying to force a few bites down.

"Jake, healing will take time, and the pain may never fully go away, but it *will* become more bearable––without alcohol. Son, you need to consider Alcoholics Anonymous. I'll help find meetings and go with you. Additionally, you should see a counselor to cope with your loss and reconnect with your daughter. Emma would have wanted you to care for her.

"We'll be at the playground next Friday around three-thirty; come see her. She'd love to spend time with her daddy," she begged. She wiped away the tears and turned, taking stock of Jake's meager kitchen supplies, and making a grocery list. "I'm going to the store. No drinking while I'm away. I won't be long."

As the door shut behind her, Jake leaned against the doorway and looked around. The stench of despair and alcohol hung heavily in the air.

His mother's stern warning echoed in his mind, her words a stark reminder of the concern etched into her aging face. She had found him in this state one too many times, and her patience was wearing thin.

Jake knew he was testing the limits of her love and understanding, and he felt a twinge of guilt for the burden he was placing on her and the rest of the family.

His thoughts drifted back to the night that had shattered his world. The car accident that claimed the lives of his Emma and their newborn son Liam. The violent collision unfolded like a surreal nightmare, a deafening symphony of twisted metal, shattering glass, and agonizing human cries.

He snatched a beer, his hands trembling

as he brought it to his lips, downing it in a single, desperate gulp. He reached for another. He could see Emma's silhouette, her face contorted in pain, the smell of smoke smothering him.

Darkness closed in around him like an ominous shroud, barring out the world in a suffocating embrace. He slid to the floor wailing like a wounded dog.

AN HOUR LATER, his mom came back, placing the bags on the table. She shook her head at the empty beer can on the counter, and another half-full in Jake's hand.

Furious, she took the can from him, emptied it down the drain, walked to the refrigerator, and proceeded to empty the rest of the beer he had stashed there.

Jake dropped into the kitchen chair and hung his head.

As she finished putting away the groceries, she hugged him tightly. "I'll see you at the playground next Friday. Please don't let Ivy down."

Chapter 2

ONCE HIS MOM was gone, Jake methodically closed all the blinds, turned out the lights, and got two beers that he had hidden in a cupboard, before sinking onto the couch. The once vibrant, happy, and warm home he and Emma built now felt desolate, shrouded in darkness, and devoid of life. The relentless grip of loneliness taunted him.

His mother's words echoed in his mind. Her repeated warnings were wake-up calls, stark reminders that he couldn't continue down this destructive path. But the pull of the bottle, the temporary relief it offered from his overwhelming grief, was difficult to resist.

He knew he needed help, but the idea of facing his pain head-on was a terrifying prospect no matter how much he wanted to make things right.

By dark, he'd downed another six beers and a couple of vodka shots. Jake began to drift into a hazy rest. He tossed and turned unable to find peace, until he gradually succumbed to a deep sleep.

Faint sounds of laughter and giggling radiated from the kitchen, memories of Emma and Ivy. Though he couldn't tell what they were doing in there, completeness filled him.

Then, he heard Emma's voice. "Jake, dinner is ready. Ivy and I fixed your favorite." Traditionally, Emma and Ivy handled dinner preparations, while Jake took the opportunity to catch up on the news. In return, he would handle the cleanup and dishwashing duties.

Jake switched off the television and made his way to the kitchen. As he entered, he reached for Ivy and twirled her around, eliciting giggles. "You know, every time I come home to you and Ivy, it feels like I'm stepping into a piece of heaven." He then took Emma into his arms, drawing her close and planting a kiss on her lips.

When they sat down for dinner, Ivy handed Jake a picture she had drawn. As he unfolded it, he saw four stick figures: Mommy, Daddy, Ivy, and a tiny additional stick figure.

He glanced at Emma. She nodded with a wide grin. "Yes, we have a baby on the way, my love."

Overwhelmed with joy, Jake rose from his chair, hugged his wife tightly, and bestowed a loving kiss on his giggling daughter's head.

"I can't believe we're going to have another little one. I'm over the moon. How are you feeling? This is just... it's incredible!" His gaze shifted between Emma and Ivy, the love for his family making his heart pound.

Jake tossed and turned on the sofa. The feeling of holding his wife and daughter, with the news of another baby on the way, filled his heart. He was ecstatic.

Part of him knew it was a dream, but he held on to it, never wanting to wake up. However, an abrupt fall from the sofa turned the elation he had just felt, into emptiness.

Collapsed on the floor, he sobbed and shouted, "Why did you have to die, Emma? I miss you so much! Your love gave me strength. I'm not sure how to move forward without you. How do I raise Ivy alone? She misses you—we both do. I know I'm failing you. I'm so lost without you. Please, please, please forgive me." His words were punctuated by sobs, his heart felt shattered, and a profound ache consumed the pit of his stomach.

Hours later, Jake crawled back onto the sofa, where he stared at the ceiling, the echoes of his dream still resonating in his mind. His pain was raw. He couldn't escape the torment.

Jake lost the greatest love he'd ever

known, his heart torn apart by the excruciating pain of her absence, leaving him hollow, lost in an abyss of darkness that seemed endless.

He wasn't sure he was strong enough to find his way out.

Chapter 3

ON FRIDAY, AMELIA and Ivy made their way to their favorite playground. Their arrival was punctual, three-thirty on the dot. For Ivy, it was just another enjoyable afternoon at the playground with her nana.

Ivy wasted no time and darted toward the monkey bars. The space was alive with children climbing, jumping, swinging, chatting, laughing, and occasionally shedding tears when minor mishaps occurred.

Amelia found a spot on the bench under a maple tree, the shade and breeze welcome in the afternoon heat.

Ivy had been visiting this playground for years; once upon a time with her mommy and daddy, and now with Amelia and, occasionally, papa. Over time, Ivy had transitioned from the toddler swing to the big girl swing. Amelia fondly remembered the joyous moments with Jake who would push his little girl high until she would squeal with delight.

There was also the memory of Ivy

23

sitting on his lap while they swung back and forth on the larger swings. Jake had guided her on the jungle gym and raced her down the slide to Emma waiting at the bottom.

By the time she turned five, Ivy had mastered wall climbing, the monkey bars, and relished climbing up the tube spiral slides. She insisted that going up was more fun than sliding down.

Three-thirty came and went with no sign of Jake. Although Amelia felt disappointed, her smile remained unwavering for Ivy's sake.

When they got home, Amelia prepared dinner, with Ivy eagerly helping set the table and chattered away excitedly. "Nana, what are we having for dinner? It smells really good!"

Amelia smiled. "We're having your favorite, spaghetti and meatballs."

"Yummy. Thank you, Nana. I made a new friend at the park today. We played on the swings together!" Ivy replied, carefully placing the forks beside each plate.

"That sounds wonderful, Ivy," Amelia said, her heart warmed by Ivy's happiness. "I'm glad you had fun today. Now, let's get everything ready. Dinner is almost served!"

The family enjoyed their meal together. Papa Bill took charge of doing the dishes, while Amelia read Ivy a bedtime story and kissed her goodnight.

As Amelia joined her husband in the family room, she couldn't hide her concern. "Jake's situation is getting worse. I don't know what else to do," she began, her voice laced with distress. "I went to his house this week, and it's heartbreaking. His drinking … It's out of control, and he's completely let himself and the house go. It's like he's given up since Emma passed. And he just falls apart whenever her name comes up. We need to find a way to help him, he's losing himself in his grief." Her eyes conveyed the depth of her concern, clearly troubled by her son's downward spiral.

Amelia's husband took a deep breath, turning to face her with a solemn look. "I know it's incredibly worrying. Jake's always been sensitive, and losing Emma hit him hard. Maybe it's time we consider getting him some professional help, someone who can guide him through this."

Amelia nodded, her hands clasped tightly. "I've thought about that too. But you know Jake, he's so resistant to talking to anyone about his feelings. He's closed himself off from the world."

Bill sighed, rubbing his temples. "We can't just watch him destroy himself. What if we try a different approach?

Perhaps we can talk to a counselor first, get some advice on how to approach him. We could even offer to go with him for support."

"That might work," Amelia said, a flicker of hope in her eyes. "And we need to make sure Ivy is okay through all this. She's so young, but she senses something's wrong."

He reached out, squeezing her hand gently. "We'll get through this, together. Let's take it one step at a time. First, we find a counselor and make a plan. We're a family, and we'll help Jake find his way back. He's not alone in this." His words were firm and filled with determination.

Chapter 4

JAKE WOKE FROM a nightmare. He had no idea what time it was or, for that matter, what day it was. Everything blurred into a shapeless void, and he couldn't recall his last meal.

Head pounding, he hoisted himself from the sofa, his unsteady legs carrying him to the dimly lit bathroom. Even without turning the light on, his reflection in the mirror painted a grim picture. His hair clung to his scalp, slicked with greasy neglect. His face was a shade of green that hinted at his despair. His bloodshot eyes bore the unmistakable burden of dark, sleepless nights and unremitting anguish. His clothes hung loosely, shirt slipping from his shoulders, and jeans barely clinging to his hips.

His mom's words replayed in his mind: *If you keep going like this, Ivy will lose you too...*

Was it coming to that? Was he drinking himself to death? Ivy would be an orphan.

He walked to the kitchen, bypassing the urge to grab a cold beer, and instead, busied himself with brewing a strong cup of coffee. His heart was weighed down by a mixture of emotions. Memories surged through his mind as he sipped his steaming brew.

With the coffee's warmth coursing through him, he drove to Charlotte Beach, and walked to the end of the pier where he found a spot to sit. The repetition of the waves created a soothing rhythm.

Along the way, people strolled by, some in silent contemplation, while others shared animated conversations. The passing boats glided gracefully, marking their entry into Lake Ontario from the Genesee River.

Lost in the tranquility of the scene, he lost track of time, but eventually, the sun began setting and his eyes were fixated by the gradual descent of the sun on the horizon. The sun's blazing colors were fast disappearing as it sprinted to the finish line and skillfully passed the baton to the moon.

The night air was chilly. The sky almost black, displayed strategically placed clouds that were charcoal-like. The moon revealed only a sliver of its magnificent self as if sensing the hollowness within him.

"Emma, I miss you so much," Jake whispered.

In the darkness of the night, he pictured Emma's shimmering eyes. He remembered how they blissfully danced to the beat of their heart. He remembered the tenderness of holding her through their first dance so long ago.

In the silence of the night, he could hear the echo of her laughter. Memories of him holding her through countless nights as they drifted to sleep, surrounded him.

His vision became blurry, his eyes drowned as tears fought their way out. Unable to hold them back, they came crashing down as he thought of the emptiness of a life without Emma.

He looked at their photograph now prominently displayed as his phone screensaver; she looked so alive! He caressed her scarf encircling his neck and inhaled the remnants of the smell of her.

With a deep sigh, he uttered, "I wish I may, I wish I might . . . I wish you were here my love, so I could hold you tight!" But of course, wishes didn't come true. If they did, Emma would never have died.

He headed back to his car. As he reached the parking lot, a few rows away, a commotion caught his attention. Under a light pole, some guy was attempting to wrestle a woman's purse from her grasp.

Her face etched with a mixture of terror and anger, she clutched her purse as her young daughter, no older than five, wept beside her. The little girl's voice was a heartbreaking cry for help.

Jake took off running toward them. He could hear the woman's words, a mix of defiance and distress. She was doing her best to fend off the assailant, her face determined.

The young man had a wild look in his eyes. He appeared to be oblivious to Jake approaching. Drugs? Jake sure hoped not. He hoped to talk some sense into the guy.

The woman was screaming, "Just go! Leave us alone!" Her words trembled.

Jake forced himself to slow down as he edged closer, then spoke firmly but calmly. "Hey, man, let her go. This isn't worth it."

As the attacker turned and locked eyes with Jake's firm gaze, the mother tightened her grip on her purse and swiftly reached for her daughter's hand, pulling her close. The little girl's sobs echoed through the parking lot, while her mother stood protectively by her side.

"You're scaring the little girl." Jake pulled two twenties from his pocket––beer money––but this was a better cause, and held them out. "It's all I have. Take it."

The guy tore the money from Jake's hand and bolted.

Jake knelt down in front of the little girl.

"You're safe, honey. You're safe. It's all right."

Thoughts of his daughter flooded his mind, and he felt a sharp longing rip through his gut. Here he was, playing the hero for a little girl when he'd abandoned his own. Guilt and remorse washed over him as he vowed to reconnect with Ivy. He would mend the broken bond between them, he would find the man—the father—he used to be.

Rising to his feet, Jake asked the woman if she was ok. She looked at him, her eyes convening a deep sense of gratitude.

"Thank you." She reached into her purse and pulled out a twenty-dollar bill extending it toward Jake as a token of her appreciation.

"I don't need this," he insisted firmly, yet kindly. "I was just helping out. It's what anyone should do." His voice held sincerity.

The woman seemed to pause for a moment, registering his refusal, but then she smiled softly, tucking the bill back into her purse. Turning to her daughter, she said, "Come on Willow, let's head home."

Willow turned to Jake and said, "Thank you, mister."

As they walked away, Jake watched them go, feeling a sense of fulfillment that only comes from doing the right thing, without any expectation in return.

As he watched their car drive away, a newfound sense of strength began to well up within him.

JAKE RETURNED HOME, an unwavering determination to change burned inside him. He found his way to his bedroom, where the weight of his decision sat heavily on his shoulders.

It was the first time he had ventured into that room to sleep since Emma had passed away.

As Jake sat on the edge of the bed, a torrent of thoughts and emotions overwhelmed him. In the solitude of their room, he tried to hold himself together, but the ache in his soul felt excruciating like a dagger slowly turning in his heart. His lungs forgot how to breathe, leaving him gasping for air, and his mind played cruel tricks on him.

He could still hear Emma's voice saying, "I love you."

The sound of her laughter echoed in his memory. Every touch, every kiss, every moment they had shared played clearly in his mind. He had cherished their love, thrived in its promise, and now, the emptiness without her was unbearable.

With a heavy heart, he whispered, "I wish you and our baby were here."

He lay down, and the empty space beside him served as a stark reminder of her absence.

Jake closed his eyes, took a deep breath, determined to make positive changes and honor the love and memory of his wife.

WHEN JAKE WOKE up in the morning, the sunlight streaming through the window of their once-shared room enveloped him in warmth and hope. It felt like a new beginning, a fresh start after the darkness of his past.

Determined to move forward, he took that first step, making a silent promise to himself and Emma that he would embrace the light and find a way to live again.

Chapter 5

FOLLOWING HIS FIRST night spent in their marital bed since Emma's passing, Jake awoke with a familiar craving for alcohol. However, he knew he had to resist that urge. For the sake of both his well-being and, more importantly, for the well-being of his daughter.

He had to cast aside that temptation and find a way to rebuild his life.

With his head pounding and a deep sense of regret, Jake made a pivotal decision. He acknowledged that he couldn't overcome his addiction on his own. It was time to seek professional help.

He began by researching treatment options and found a local addiction recovery center. Taking that first step was a mixture of anxiety and hope. He dialed the number, his voice shaky but resolute, and scheduled an appointment.

He reached out to his mother, thanking her, and told her he decided to get help. He added, "Mom, I'm not fooling myself into thinking this is going to be easy. I have a hard journey ahead and will need your support more than ever. I'm so grateful for all you and Dad have done for Ivy and me. Please continue to look after her until I'm strong enough to be her dad again. Tell her that I love her so much."

His mom's tear-filled voice broke his heart. "We love you and I'm proud of you for taking this first step son."

JAKE CHECKED INTO the recovery center, and his journey was nothing short of agonizing. The severity of his alcohol addiction became painfully apparent. The initial hours were the worst; withdrawal symptoms hit him like a freight train. Intense cravings clawed at his every thought, his body drenched in sweat as he wrestled with the decision to give in or fight through the torment. But Jake was determined to break free from the chains of addiction.

As the days turned into weeks, Jake started to regain his clarity of mind and a sense of control over his life. His determination gradually guided him towards the path of sobriety and a new chance at life.

Sixty days later, Jake attended his first AA meeting with mixed emotions, not knowing what to expect. But he found solace in hearing the stories of others who had walked a similar path, and he realized he wasn't alone in his journey.

Jake embraced the Twelve Steps of AA. He secured a sponsor and began working through the steps with guidance. He understood that sobriety was a lifelong commitment, and he was determined to rebuild his life for himself but mostly for Ivy.

JAKE BEGAN THE reacquaintance process with his precious daughter. He had longed to be her dad again but now that it was time, he was filled with a mix of emotions: anticipation, anxiety, but, above all, love.

The day he saw Ivy again was a sunny, clear afternoon. The air felt crisp, and the world seemed brighter and more vibrant than it had in a long time. As he approached his parents' home, he could hardly contain his excitement.

As his mother opened the front door, there she was, his little girl, standing with a mix of curiosity and apprehension.

Jake knelt down, extending his arms as he called out to her. "Ivy, my sweet girl, I've missed you so much!"

Ivy's eyes widened, and then, with an excited burst of energy, she dashed toward him. "Daddy!" her voice filled with joy. "I've missed you too."

Their hug was a heartfelt collision

of love and longing, a testament to the unbreakable bond between father and daughter.

Tears welled up in Jake's eyes as he held Ivy close. "I promise, Daddy will be better for you," he whispered, his voice thick with emotion.

He was acutely aware of the time he had missed with her, but he was determined to make amends and create new, beautiful memories together. Ivy, in her innocence and purity, showed no judgment, only joy, and love for her father.

Amelia, standing at the doorway, watched the reunion with a mixture of relief and concern. After a moment, she approached Jake, her expression softening. "Jake, seeing you with Ivy... it's a reminder of what's truly important. We've been worried about you."

Jake looked up meeting her eyes. "I know, Mom. I'm trying, really. It's just been so hard without Emma. I know I've got a lot to make up for. I'm sorry for everything."

His mother nodded, a small smile tugging at the corners of her quivering lips. "It's a start, Jake. Just being here now means a lot. We've all missed you."

Jake nodded, squeezing Ivy a little tighter.

OVER THE DAYS, weeks, months that followed, Jake and Ivy slowly but steadily rekindled their bond. Each day brought new opportunities for bonding and healing. They played games, read stories, and laughed together. Ivy's infectious laughter and boundless enthusiasm helped mend the cracks in Jake's heart, filling them with newfound hope and happiness. Her enthusiasm for even the smallest things––a butterfly in the garden, a rainbow after the rain––reawakened a sense of wonder in him that he thought he had lost.

Ivy's unconditional love and acceptance showed Jake that, despite his past mistakes, there was a path to redemption and joy. In her eyes, he wasn't just her father; he was her hero, her playmate, her storyteller–roles he embraced with gratitude that filled him with a newfound purpose and determination to be the best version of himself, for her, and for himself.

Jake knew that he had a second chance to be the father Ivy needed and deserved. He was committed to making the most of this opportunity, ensuring that the dark days of his addiction would remain in the past and that their future would be filled with love, laughter, and a bond that nothing could sever.

After spending a few months re-establishing their bond, Ivy and Jake visited the cemetery, bringing flowers to Emma's resting place. Then finally it was time for Ivy to go home with her dad.

Chapter 6

THE PROSPECT OF returning to his old job as a firefighter filled Jake with a sense of both excitement and trepidation. It was a crucial step on his journey to rebuild his life, and it meant a return to the sense of purpose and community that had once been so important to him.

He walked into the captain's office, his heart pounding with a blend of enthusiasm and nervousness. "Captain Martinez," Jake greeted, trying to sound more confident than he felt.

The captain looked up from his desk, his expression serious but not unkind. "Jake, good to see you. Have a seat. Are you feeling ready to come back?"

Jake nodded, taking a deep breath. " I am, Captain. I've been working hard to get back to where I need to be, mentally and physically. Being a firefighter... it's a big part of who I am. I've missed it."

Captain Martinez leaned back in his chair, observing Jake closely. "It's not just about being physically fit, Jake. This job... it demands a lot mentally and emotionally.

Are you sure you're up for it? We can't have any doubts when we're out there in the field."

Jake met his gaze squarely. "I understand the concerns, and I don't take them lightly. I've been through a lot, but I've also been getting help, working through things. I want to be here, to be part of the team again. I know it won't be easy, but I'm committed to doing whatever it takes."

Captain Martinez nodded slowly. "Alright. We'll start you on a trial basis, see how it goes. We're a team here, and we look out for each other. If you're ready to be part of that again, we're ready to have you back."

Jake felt a surge of relief and gratitude. "Thank you, Captain. I won't let you down."

As he left the office, Jake felt a renewed sense of purpose. The road ahead would be challenging, but he was ready to face it head-on, knowing that reclaiming his place at the firehall was a vital part of his journey to rebuild his life.

JAKE'S DAYS BEGAN early, just as they always had when he was a firefighter. The piercing sound of the alarm clock jolted him out of sleep. He'd slip out of bed and, with a sense of renewed determination, go through his morning routine with the precision and discipline he had always maintained.

As he put on his uniform, he couldn't help but feel a surge of pride. But there was something even more significant than his career that was at the forefront of his mind––the daily presence of his daughter.

He woke Ivy from sleep with a gentle shake. Together, they'd share a quick breakfast, during which Jake would pack her school lunch with her favorite snacks and a heartfelt note of encouragement. He valued these moments of togetherness, a far cry from the distance that had once separated them.

The firehouse had always been a second home for Jake, a place where camaraderie and a shared sense of purpose ran deep. He returned to a welcoming group of colleagues, many of whom had stood by him during his battle with alcoholism. Their support was a testament to the bonds formed in the line of duty.

The routines and the rush of firefighting were familiar, and they provided Jake with a sense of grounding. The adrenaline of responding to emergencies, the training drills, and the ever-present camaraderie helped him rebuild not only his career but his sense of self as well.

EVERY DAY AFTER school, Ivy would eagerly recount her day to her father. Evenings were dedicated to family dinners. It was a time to connect, to talk about the day's events. The dinner table became another place of bonding, laughter, and the creation of cherished memories.

During one of their dinners, as they were passing around dishes and settling into the comfortable routine of their evening meal, Ivy looked up excitedly.

"Daddy, guess what we did at school today?" she exclaimed, her eyes sparkling with enthusiasm.

Jake, intrigued, smiled at her. "What did you do?"

"We learned about the solar system in science class!" Ivy said, her voice filled with wonder. "Did you know that Saturn has rings made of ice and rock? And Jupiter is so big, you could fit all the other planets inside it!"

"That's amazing," Jake replied, genuinely impressed. "You're becoming quite the little scientist. What's your favorite planet?"

Ivy thought for a moment, her brow furrowed in concentration. "I think... Mars! Because it's red and maybe there were even aliens there!"

Jake laughed, delighted by her

imagination. "Mars, huh? Maybe one day you'll be an astronaut and explore it yourself."

Ivy's eyes lit up at the idea. "That would be so cool!"

As they continued their dinner, the conversation flowed easily, filled with more stories from Ivy's school day and shared plans for the coming weekend.

As the night wound down, Jake sat on Ivy's bed, reading her favorite bedtime stories.

THE DAYS TURNED into weeks and the weeks into months. For Jake and Ivy, it was a journey of healing, rebuilding, and rediscovery. Their home was no longer filled with the dark shadows of the past, but rather with the warmth of their shared moments.

The fire within him was rekindled, but this time, it was a fire of hope, love, and second chances. Together, they were writing a new chapter in their lives, one filled with the embers of a fresh start and the promise of a brighter tomorrow.

Ivy and Jake restarted their frequent visits to the playground, becoming regulars. On this particular day, Jake sat peacefully at a picnic table, observing his daughter as she eagerly tackled the various challenges the space offered. He marveled at her mastery of the monkey bars, a feat she accomplished after triumphantly scaling the climbing wall.

Ivy had her fair share of friends here, some she had known for years from their playground visits, and others she had met at school. She was a bundle of energy, with her long blonde hair, sparkling brown eyes, a smattering of freckles on her cheeks, a few missing teeth, and a smile that could light up the world.

As they drove home, Jake and Ivy stopped at the village ice cream stand. When they approached the counter, Jake turned to Ivy with a knowing smile. "I bet you're going to choose vanilla, right? Your favorite!" he said, ready to order for her.

Ivy wrinkled her nose and shook her head. "Actually, Daddy, I like chocolate now. It's my new favorite!"

Jake looked surprised but quickly recovered with a chuckle. "Chocolate, huh? Well, that's a change! When did this happen?"

"Just a few months ago," Ivy replied with a grin. "I tried it at a friend's birthday party and loved it!"

"Alright then, one chocolate ice cream for the young lady," Jake said to the server, smiling at Ivy. "And I'll have the same. It's about time I caught up with your new favorites."

As they sat enjoying their ice creams, Jake realized how much Ivy was growing and changing, and he made a mental note to keep up with her evolving tastes and interests. It was a small but significant reminder of the joys and surprises of parenting.

When they got home, Jake prepared a dinner of stir-fried chicken strips, tater tots, and a small salad for both of them. After their meal, they followed their new evening ritual, looking through photographs and taking turns reading to each other.

Later, Jake tucked her in. "Sweet dreams, my girl. I love you infinitely."

"I love you the mostest, Daddy."

They blew each other kisses and in unison whispered, "Good night."

Chapter 7

AROUND MID-MORNING, THE first emergency call of the day came in, alerting the team to a fire at a local warehouse. As the alarm sounded, the firefighters sprang into action.

"Let's move, team! Gear up!" Captain Martinez barked.

Jake, pulling on his protective gear, turned to his colleague, Mike. "Looks like a big one. Ready to tackle this?"

Mike nodded, securing his helmet. "Born ready. Let's make sure we get everyone out safe." As the fire truck sped towards the scene, the team coordinated their approach.

"Remember, keep communication lines open and watch each other's backs in there," Captain Martinez reminded them over the roar of the engine.

Arriving at the warehouse, they were greeted by thick, black smoke and intense heat. Jake and his team immediately got to work, unfurling hoses and strategizing their entry.

"Jake, Mike, take the east side! The rest

of you, with me to the main entrance," directed the captain.

The firefighters battled the flames relentlessly, the heat and smoke a formidable adversary. Despite the challenging conditions, they worked efficiently, ensuring the safe evacuation of everyone in the building.

After hours of hard work, the fire was finally under control. Exhausted but relieved, the team gathered outside the charred remains of the warehouse.

"We did good today, team," Captain Martinez said, looking at each of his firefighters with pride. "No lives lost, thanks to your efforts."

Jake, removing his helmet and wiping the soot from his face, exchanged a tired but satisfied glance with Mike. "Another day, another save," Mike said.

"Yeah," Jake replied, feeling a deep sense of fulfillment. "That's what we're here for."

Later in the afternoon, the second emergency call came in.

Jake and his fellow firefighters rushed to the scene of a car accident, their sirens wailing. As they arrived, they were met with a disturbing sight: a mangled car, its front end crushed, smoke rising from the engine.

Jake's mind involuntarily rewinds to the sounds of the car crash that took his wife's life. This haunting flashback was persistent, a cutting reminder of the grief and guilt he carried underscoring his role as a firefighter.

The vehicle had crashed into a concrete barrier on the side of the highway, the impact so severe that the engine compartment was pushed into the driver's seat. Inside, they found a young driver, bloodied and disoriented, with a shattered windshield and airbags deployed. The driver had been texting, a stark reminder of how quickly life can be altered in an instant.

Later that week, Jake had to testify as an expert witness regarding a devastating house fire he and his team had responded to. The fire had claimed the life of one of the residents.

Exiting the courtroom, Jake's thoughts still lingered on his testimony–*A scorched body and the carcass of the dog by her side.*

His mind wandered as he walked, causing him to collide with a woman, nearly toppling her over. Files flew everywhere and scattered on the ground. Jake began apologizing while gathering the documents.

Retrieving the last file, he stood, ready to hand it back to the person he had bumped into. Facing him, a woman waited with crossed arms and an unamused expression.

Jake stammered, "I am so, so sorry. I wasn't paying attention to where I was going. Are you okay? Did I hurt you?"

"No! You've done enough. Thanks for gathering the files, but I'm in a hurry. Next time, pay attention to where you're going." She briskly walked away.

As she disappeared into a courtroom, Jake had a sudden recollection—parking lot, purse, a bewildered young man, the little girl––Willow. This was the woman who had almost been robbed of her purse at Charlotte Beach. *The fear on Willow's face––wanting to protect her––my turning point!'*

Jake patiently waited, and after a lengthy court session, she emerged and quickly made her way towards the exit. Jake followed her, and as they stepped outside, she glanced at him.

"Hey, are you stalking me? I wouldn't recommend it. I know most of the police officers around here. Besides, you've already tried to knock me over, and that didn't work; that should tell you something."

Jake chuckled and tried to keep up with her. "I just want to apologize."

"OK . . . apology accepted. Now, have a great day, sir."

He grinned at her abrupt dismissal but he wasn't done. "Do you have time for a cup of coffee? It's the least you can do, after what I did for you. By the way, my name is Jake Donovan."

Confusion wrinkled her brow. "What do you mean *the least I can do for you*? You're the one who almost knocked me over. Thanks, but no thanks. I have a busy day ahead." She quickened her pace.

"Are you Willow's mom?"

She turned to him, bewildered. "How do you know Willow?"

"I don't. We met once, but never got your name. I tried to intervene when a man was trying to take your purse up at Charlotte." He smirked and continued, "I did save your life you know? If I hadn't intervened, you never know what that guy would have done."

She looked embarrassed. "I didn't recognize you. Thank you. You looked like you had crawled out of a hellhole that day. You clean up decently. And by the way, you did not save my life."

"Well, I can explain my appearance that day."

She extended her hand. "I'm Tiana Williams. Nice to meet you, Jake Donovan. I really do have a busy day ahead. Thank you again for what you did."

Jake was struck by the remarkable

combination of determination and self-assurance she displayed as she made her way to her office.

Chapter 8

TODAY MARKED THE one-year anniversary of Emma's passing. Jake and Ivy planned a heartfelt journey of remembrance and love. They began with a visit to her resting place, leaving fresh flowers and sitting in quiet reflection.

Later, they visited their cherished restaurant for breakfast, ordering Emma's favorite dishes including her much-loved pancakes. As they waited for their food, Jake reminisced about Emma's unique way of eating them.

"You know, Ivy, your mom had this funny way of eating pancakes," Jake said with a smile. "She would roll them up and then dip them in her coffee."

Ivy made a face. "Yucky! Pancakes in coffee?"

Jake laughed. "I know, right? I thought the same thing. But she loved it. Said it was the perfect combination."

Their food arrived, and as Jake demonstrated how Emma used to eat her pancakes, Ivy giggled uncontrollably. "That's so weird, Daddy!"

"Yeah, it was one of her quirky habits," Jake said, chuckling along with Ivy.

Then, Ivy's expression turned curious. "Did Mom like any other weird foods?"

Jake thought for a moment, then his face lit up. "Oh, she loved peanut butter with pickles. Can you imagine that?"

"Eww, that sounds even weirder!" Ivy exclaimed, scrunching up her nose, which sent them both into another round of laughter.

Returning home, they planted a memorial oak tree in their backyard, symbolizing growth, strength, and enduring love.

In the comfort of their living room, they watched a favorite movie, and sifted through treasured photographs, reliving precious moments. To conclude their day, Ivy and Jake made their way to Braddock's Bay, and released two balloons to honor the memory of their beloved mother and wife.

As they stood side by side, facing the open expanse of the bay, Jake looked down at Ivy. "Do you want to say something as we let these go?" he asked gently.

Ivy nodded, her eyes fixed on the balloons. She took a deep breath and said, "To Mommy and baby Liam, up in heaven. We miss you and love you. This is for you."

Jake felt a lump form in his throat as he joined in, "Emma, every day you're in our hearts. We're sending these to you and Liam with all our love."

Together, they released the balloons, watching as they ascended higher and higher, their colors vibrant against the sky. They stood in silence, holding hands, as the balloons drifted out of sight, feeling a sense of peace and connection with Emma and Liam.

It was a bittersweet day; blending sorrow and affection, allowing Jake and Ivy to remember and celebrate Emma and Liam, while progressing on their path toward healing.

TIANA WILLIAMS WAS a dedicated attorney who made it her mission to advocate for children. She graduated with honors from NYU / Law, where she honed her legal skills and deepened her commitment to child welfare. Her tireless dedication to her young clients was evident in her relentless work ethic, spending long hours at her desk, pouring over case files and legislation to ensure the best outcomes for the children she represented.

Today Tiana and Willow strolled through the rows of pumpkins at Kelly's farm, enjoying the crisp autumn air and the vibrant colors of the season.

Willow carefully selected her favorite one to carve for Halloween. "Mommy, look at this one!" she exclaimed, pointing to a large, perfectly round pumpkin.

Tiana walked over and examined the pumpkin that had caught Willow's attention. "Wow, that is a great find, Willow! It's almost as big as you are!" she said with a chuckle.

Willow beamed with pride. "It's perfect for our jack-o'-lantern. Can we get it, please?"

"Of course, we can," Tiana replied, smiling at her daughter's excitement. "This will make a fantastic jack-o'-lantern for our porch."

Together, they carefully picked up the pumpkin, placing it in their cart. Satisfied with their find, they made their way to the farm's cozy café where they treated themselves to some freshly made donuts and steaming cups of hot chocolate. As they sat at a wooden picnic table, Tiana noticed Jake and she waved.

"Miss Williams! Long time no see. How have you been?" Jake called out in a cheerful tone silently hoping she would stay and chat a bit.

"Hi, Jake. Everything's good, just trying to enjoy the fall season. How about you?"

Jake smiled. "We're doing well too. We couldn't resist coming here for some pumpkin picking and sweet treats. This is my daughter Ivy. Is that Willow with you?"

"Nice to meet you Ivy, and yes, this is my daughter Willow." Tiana gestured to the young girl by her side. "We've been having a great time finding the perfect pumpkin and enjoying the day."

"It's nice to meet you, Willow," Jake said with a friendly nod toward her, glad the girl didn't remember him from their 'first' meeting.

Tiana and Jake found themselves in a pleasant, casual conversation and the girls excitedly shared their pumpkin choices and plans for carving. While sipping their hot chocolate, they discussed their favorite fall traditions and their kids' activities.

As they said their goodbyes Jake teased Tiana, "You still owe me a coffee."

She laughed with such genuine abandon, a reflection of her authenticity, with no pretense. Jake decided then and there he was going to see more of Tiana Williams.

Chapter 9

THE HOLIDAY SEASON was fast approaching, and Jake was determined to make it memorable for Ivy. Together, they decided to head to Cobblestone Farm to pick out a perfect Christmas tree. As they explored the rows of evergreens, Jake was surprised to run into Tiana and Willow.

Jake greeted them with a friendly smile. "We have to stop meeting like this. Purse snatching, pumpkins, and now trees."

Tiana smiled. "Jake, Ivy, what a wonderful coincidence!"

"We're here to pick out a beautiful Christmas tree for Ivy and me to decorate."

Ivy chimed in, "My mom used to join us for the tree cutting. This is our favorite place, but this year, it's just Daddy and me."

Tiana nodded. "Ivy, sometimes different is ok. You and your dad can create your own special holiday traditions. And so can you and your mom."

Ivy, her voice tinged with sadness,

replied, "My mom died. I really miss her."

Tiana's heart ached for Jake and his little girl. She assumed he was divorced. "Oh, I'm so sorry to hear that." She knelt and hugged Ivy then looked at Jake and whispered, "I'm sorry."

They strolled through the farm, and the two families decided to make the experience even more enjoyable by assisting each other in cutting down their chosen trees.

When they were all set to leave with their trees, Jake turned to Tiana. "How about you and I grab a cup of coffee one of these days? I'd like to see you."

She looked embarrassed and offered an alternative idea. "Willow and I are planning to go ice skating at Manhattan Square Park on New Year's Eve. If you and Ivy would like to join us, we'll treat you to some hot chocolate. I might even bring some of my homemade cookies."

Jake appreciated the invitation and nodded. "That sounds like a terrific plan. We'd be delighted to join you. "

Ivy and Willow excitedly chattered about the upcoming ice-skating plans on New Year's Eve. As they began to leave Jake called out, "Merry Christmas."

A few days later, he arranged for Ivy to visit the fire station. She beamed with pride as she met his teammates, explored the impressive fire trucks, and learned about the lifesaving work her daddy did.

As Christmas drew near, Jake organized a surprise visit from Santa Claus to their home. Ivy's eyes lit up with wonder as Santa handed her a gift, and they all shared stories and laughter. It was a magical evening that neither Ivy nor Jake would soon forget.

DESPITE HER BUSY schedule, Tiana and Willow spent a weekend decorating their home. They strung lights, hung ornaments, and laughed as they placed the star atop the Christmas tree. Then they took a moment to admire their work. Tiana turned to Willow, her eyes twinkling with the reflection of the Christmas lights.

"What's your favorite decoration we put up this year, Willow?"

Willow glanced around, her eyes lingering on the various ornaments and lights. "I love the lights the most, Mommy. They make our home look like a fairyland," she replied, her face lit up with a bright smile.

Tiana nodded. "The lights are magical, aren't they? My favorite decoration is the angel you made for me with your picture on it. When I place it on our tree, it reminds me of how grateful I am for you, sweetie." Their home was now filled with the warm glow of holiday cheer.

Then they helped pack food boxes for a local shelter, and Willow experienced the joy of giving to others. Tiana's dedication to teaching her daughter the value of compassion was evident.

Tiana said, "Willow, always remember that being kind and giving to others is one of the most important things we can do in life. It's not just about what we have, but what we share with others that truly matters. When we give, we not only help those in need, but we also nurture our hearts."

Willow listened intently, and Tiana continued, "In a world that can sometimes seem big and complicated, our acts of kindness are like ripples on a pond. They spread far and wide, touching more lives than we can see. So, always carry kindness in your heart, sweetheart, and remember that even a little bit of help can do big things."

Tiana's words were simple yet profound, planting a seed of empathy in Willow's young heart, a lesson that would stay with her as she grew.

ON NEW YEAR'S Eve, Tiana and Jake were meeting at Manhattan Square Park for their ice-skating adventure. This was a tradition Tiana cherished, one she and

Willow looked forward to every year.

Willow, with a beaming smile, eagerly laced up her skates. Tiana held her hand as they glided onto the ice, Willow's laughter filling the air as they twirled and swayed together.

"Look at us, Mommy! We're like ice princesses!" Willow exclaimed, her eyes shining with excitement.

Tiana laughed, joining in her daughter's imaginative play. "Yes, we are, my little ice princess. Just watch how gracefully you can glide!"

MEANWHILE, IVY'S EXCITEMENT was just as palpable. She couldn't wait to join the fun on the ice. As they stepped onto the rink, Ivy's face lit up with glee, her confidence growing with each glide and turn.

"You're doing great, Ivy!" Jake encouraged, keeping close to her.

Just then, Jake attempted a slightly more ambitious turn and slipped, landing on the ice with a thud. Ivy burst into laughter, her hand covering her mouth.

"Are you okay, Daddy?" she asked between giggles.

Jake, unharmed and chuckling, picked himself up. "I'm fine! I guess I'm not

quite the expert skater I thought I was,"

he joked, brushing the ice off his pants.

As they continued to skate, their laughter made the happy mood around them even more cheerful.

After skating, Tiana, Jake, and the girls gathered at a charming little kiosk near the rink. With flushed cheeks from the cold and hearts warmed by the evening's activities, they enjoyed cups of hot chocolate and treated themselves to homemade Christmas cookies that Tiana had baked.

Ivy's eyes lit up at the sight of the assortment of cookies, she took a bite and said, "Wow, these cookies are so good! They're even better than the ones we make, right, Daddy?"

Jake, tasting a cookie himself, agreed with a smile. "You're right, Ivy. Tiana, these are amazing. Our Christmas cookies don't even come close to these!"

Ivy nodded enthusiastically. "Yeah, we'll have to up our game next Christmas, Daddy!" Their laughter and lighthearted banter added to the cozy atmosphere.

Willow and Ivy chatted, sharing their experiences on the ice, and the parents exchanged stories of their children's progress.

In the course of their conversation, Tiana discovered that Jake worked as a firefighter and that his wife had passed away nearly two years prior. Even in their limited interactions, she could see what a caring and considerate father he was to Ivy. It was evident he made an effort to be empathetic and sensitive to Ivy's feelings about her mother's passing, trying his best to provide support and fill the emotional void left by her absence.

"So, you're a firefighter? That must be quite a demanding job."

Jake nodded, a hint of pride in his tone. "Yes, it's demanding but also very rewarding. Every day is different, and knowing that we can make a difference, keeps me going."

"That's really admirable," Tiana responded with genuine respect. "How do you balance such a challenging job with being there for Ivy, especially after such a significant loss?"

Jake sighed softly. "It's not always easy, but I've been fortunate to have a strong support system. My parents have been incredible, and I try to make the most of the time I have with her. We've been learning to navigate this new normal together."

Ivy excitedly shared with Willow her recent adventure, a tour of the firehouse where her father worked. To Ivy, it was an experience straight out of a childhood dream. She described the moment they entered the firehouse, the big red doors, the enormous bay, where towering fire trucks stood, each gleaming with a coat of vibrant red paint.

As they all savored the moment, it became clear that this gathering had brought two acquaintances and their families together, creating a beautiful conncction on a magical New Year's Eve.

The evening left a lasting impression and the possibility of new beginnings.

Chapter 10

IN THE MIDDLE of January, Jake decided to reach out to Tiana. He left her a voicemail. "Hi, Tiana, it's Jake. I got another subpoena for a court case soon. If you're available, we can grab something to eat after my court duties."

Tiana listened to his message and felt a sense of empathy for what Jake was going through. She promptly returned his call. "Hi Jake. I got your message. I think meeting for breakfast sounds like a great idea. It'll give you a good start before your court proceedings."

They met at the 'Legal Grounds Café,' conveniently situated near the courthouse and Tiana's office. Jake initiated the conversation with a warm tone. "Ivy and I had a blast ice skating with you and Willow. After enjoying your cookies, Ivy insisted that she and I should consider taking a cookie-baking class before we attempt to make them again next Christmas."

Tiana smiled, recalling the enjoyable day. "Yes, it was a lot of fun. Willow hasn't stopped talking about Ivy's vivid description of the firehouse tour. She did an exceptional job bringing her experience to life."

As they placed their breakfast orders, they engaged in light conversation. Finally, Tiana's curiosity got the best of her, and she delicately broached a sensitive topic. "I know you lost your wife almost two years ago. I'm genuinely sorry for your loss. Would you be comfortable sharing how she passed away?"

The two acquaintances and their growing bond, found themselves delving into a more personal and heartfelt conversation as they sat in the relaxed café.

With a deep sigh, Jake began to recount the untimely and tragic death of his beloved wife. "We welcomed Ivy into our lives a year after our marriage. A few years later, we decided it was time to expand our family. Our joy was immeasurable, and Ivy was over the moon knowing she would soon have a little brother. Our son, Liam, was born; we named him after my father, William."

Jake paused, his voice quivering, and he took a sip of his now cold coffee to collect himself. "I drove them home from the hospital. It was a moment of unparalleled happiness. Emma was my perfect partner, and our son was perfect, too. We were heading home together. However, on our way home, another car T-boned us on the passenger side, where Emma was sitting. I woke up in the hospital a few days later, only to receive the devastating news that both Emma and Liam had been killed in the crash.

"I sustained multiple fractures in my ribs, as well as both legs and an arm. Additionally, I suffered a severe head injury, which resulted in a concussion that caused me to lose consciousness. I underwent a series of surgeries to repair the fractures and my head injury required close monitoring. The hospital stay lasted for several weeks, and my physical condition slowly improved through intensive physical therapy.

"Counseling and emotional support were offered to assist me in coping with the trauma and grief, but I refused both, struggling with guilt for surviving while Emma and baby Liam were lost to us. The weight of this guilt still torments me."

His eyes welled up with tears, and Tiana reached out to hold his hand, offering silent support and comfort. Sensing the depth of his grief, she softly interjected, "Jake, I can't even begin to imagine how hard this must have been for you. You're incredibly strong to have come this far." Her words, filled with empathy and kindness, provided a gentle reassurance in the midst of his heartbreaking retelling of his past.

As she touched his hand, something within him shifted. It was as though the act of sharing these painful memories was cathartic, a way to unburden his heart. The process of opening up about the loss of his wife and precious son, while intensely emotional, brought a sense of release. With Tiana's understanding presence and her comforting touch on his hand, he felt compelled to continue. In his own way, he was finding a sense of liberation in the act of sharing his story. He took a deep breath and continued with the rest of his narrative, each word a step toward healing and understanding.

"I took an extended leave from my job and took refuge in the numbing embrace of alcohol and the isolation of solitude to cope with the profound pain and loss. Ivy went to live with my parents during this tumultuous period. I couldn't bear the daily reminder of Emma in her innocent eyes, and it felt as though a piece of my world had been irrevocably shattered. I let myself spiral, losing all sense of self-care and self-worth as if life had lost its meaning.

"My family made countless attempts to break through the barriers of grief that had consumed me. They implored me to recognize the toll my self-destructive behavior was taking on my daughter. Despite their efforts, I remained trapped in a cycle of despair.

"Then, one fateful late afternoon, I found myself at Charlotte, sitting at the pier, where the setting sun across the water, painted the sky with vibrant colors. I reflected on the desolate path my life had taken and the void left by Emma and Liam. As the sky darkened, I decided to leave. When I reached the parking lot, I heard a sudden commotion. I saw an attempted purse snatching unfold, and in that chaotic moment, I crossed paths with you and Willow.

"When the thief fled, leaving behind a frightened and tearful Willow, I knelt by her side. Her distress mirrored the anguish I imagined Ivy must have been enduring in my absence. It was a poignant and transformative moment. In that instance, I made a resolute decision to reclaim my life and be there for Ivy."

A bittersweet smile graced his face as he spoke, his voice carrying a mix of emotions.

"You know, Tiana," he began, "I've come to realize that you and Willow were the ones who saved my life." His words were filled with gratitude and deep appreciation. "That day in the parking lot, you two marked the beginning of my path to change things, to escape the darkness that had gripped me for so long."

Tiana, obviously touched by his acknowledgment, responded gently, "Jake, knowing that Willow and I could help you in any way means a lot to us. It's incredible how life brings people together at the right time." Her words echoed understanding and a shared recognition of their unexpected but significant impact on each other's lives.

Chapter 11

JAKE AND TIANA maintained regular contact after their breakfast encounter and talked with each other about once a week. During one of these conversations, Tiana brought up a request.

"I was wondering if you would consider giving Willow a tour of the firehouse. I think she'd absolutely love it."

Jake's response was filled with enthusiasm. "Of course, I'd be thrilled to do that. Do you have a specific day in mind that would work for you?"

Tiana quickly suggested, "How about a Saturday morning? We can all have lunch afterward, and the girls can compare notes about their experiences."

Jake was on board with the idea. "That sounds like a fantastic plan. Let's shoot for next Saturday. Would it work if I picked you and Willow up, and we can all drive there together?"

Tiana readily agreed to the arrangement, and plans were set in motion for their get-together.

JAKE TOOK A curious and wide-eyed Willow on a magical tour of the firehouse. She had heard so much from Ivy. With his protective gear in hand, he crouched down to her eye level, making her feel safe.

He spoke to her in a comforting tone, explaining the important role of firefighters and the incredible machines they used to save the day.

Their tour was marked by the blaring sound of the firehouse bell, and Jake gently covered her ears and then explained its purpose. They reached the iconic fire pole, and he let her watch in awe as one of his colleagues gracefully descended, laughter in his eyes.

The tour concluded in the cozy kitchen, where they shared cookies with Ivy and Tiana. It was a tour that ignited her curiosity. They left the firehouse smiling and headed to lunch.

Over lunch, Willow and Ivy's curiosity about the firehouse led to a barrage of questions for Jake. Their interest was boundless, and they hung on to every word of his stories.

As the meal progressed, Tiana suggested, " How about you come over to my house and we spend the rest of the day together?"

The suggestion was met with enthusiastic nods and smiles.

"That sounds like a great idea," Jake replied, the others chiming in with their agreement.

TIANA LIVED IN a charming three-bedroom brick ranch nestled near Highland Park, a pretty neighborhood. Her home was a cozy haven, and the kitchen had recently undergone a stylish renovation, making it spacious and inviting.

Willow and Ivy decided to watch "Frozen II." Although they had seen it countless times, the allure of the enchanting characters and the mesmerizing songs kept them coming back.

Tiana lovingly set up the girls on her plush sofa, placed a cozy blanket over their legs, and handed them a bowl of popcorn.

With the girls happily engrossed in the movie, Tiana and Jake retreated to her welcoming kitchen. The aroma of freshly brewed coffee filled the air as they settled at the kitchen table.

She handed him a cup and laughed. "Here's your coffee. Hopefully, that will take care of the debt of you saving my life."

Jake chuckled. They embarked on a long conversation. "So, how did you choose child advocacy law as your career?" he inquired, eager to learn more about Tiana's profession and passions.

She giggled and said, "Well, you couldn't have kicked things off with a simple 'What's your go-to comfort food?' or 'Are you a die-hard Buffalo Bills fan?'"

He laughed. "What is your favorite food, and are you a Bills fan?"

"Let's see, favorite food is mashed potatoes with bacon, chives and cream cheese, and I like the Bills although I don't spend much time watching football."

He sipped his coffee, and remarked with a smirk, "Delicious coffee! Debt settled! Now, let's circle back to my initial question. Child advocacy seems like one of those profoundly emotional and heart-wrenching jobs, although it must be incredibly fulfilling when everything falls into place. What led you to choose law as your career?"

Tiana sat up straight on her chair and started. "My mother lived in a small town on the outskirts of Rochester. She found herself facing an unexpected pregnancy and the situation was further complicated by the fact that my father was black. Her family, deeply religious and holding traditional and some antiquated beliefs, was unable to reconcile their convictions with her pregnancy, especially given the interracial aspect of her child.

"She was ousted from her family and left to navigate the harsh realities of life on the streets. She struggled to find work, taking on any job she could find, all while holding tightly to the life growing inside her.

"I remember her telling me that her love for me was the sole source of light in her otherwise bleak world. But the streets were unforgiving, and she fell into the grip of addiction as she tried to provide for us. My father, or as I like to call him 'the sperm donor' disappeared from her life after she told him she was pregnant.

"In the midst of her addiction, her ability to care for me was compromised. When I was about nine, she overdosed in a rundown drug house one day, teetering on the brink of life and death. She survived, but Child Protective Services intervened and took me into their custody. But she was determined to get her life back on track and reunite with me again someday. She embarked on the challenging path to get cleaned up, but despite her best efforts, the legal system posed significant obstacles to regaining custody.

"Tragically, she succumbed to the weight of her past mistakes. In a moment of despair, she overdosed again and died, her life cut short." There was a minute of somber silence.

Jake, deeply moved, responded. "Tiana, that's an incredibly tough road you've been through. Losing your mom in such circumstances. I can't even imagine how hard that must have been for you. It shows remarkable strength that you've come this far, despite such challenges."

"Thank you. It's been a long, harsh road, full of ups and downs. But it's made me who I am today." Her voice held a note of resilience, ready to delve further into her past.

"As an orphan, I faced a variety of experiences within the foster care system, from nurturing and caring foster families to those who were less supportive and affectionate. It was a challenging journey, marked by the scars of being the child of drugged-up parents.

"I was never adopted, and it wasn't until I reached the age of seventeen that I finally left the last foster family I had been living with for about six years. My experience there was nothing short of a real-life horror story. My foster mother epitomized what I believed a woman should never be—submissive to the core. Her husband was a sleazy, disgusting, pig and I could recount a multitude of nightmarish experiences from that house.

"During my early teens, I made a solemn

promise to myself that I would rise above the squalor of my past and pursue an education, ultimately dedicating my life to helping those who were unable to help themselves. And so, I find myself today, doing my utmost to advocate for children in any way I can."

Jake gazed at Tiana with a sense of admiration. She appeared incredibly self-assured, composed, and almost impervious to the world. It dawned on him that this seemingly impenetrable exterior might be the protective barrier she had constructed, safeguarding herself from further hurt and pain, after enduring so much hardship in her life.

He rose from his chair and positioned himself in front of her, saying, "I'd like to give you a hug."

She too stood up, and as their embrace unfolded, she melted into the refuge within his arms.

Chapter 12

As IVY AND Willow chatted excitedly about their time together, they both looked up at their parents, eager and hopeful.

"Can we do this again soon?" Ivy asked, her eyes pleading.

Willow chimed in, "Yeah, can we, Mommy?"

Tiana and Jake exchanged a glance, smiling at the children's enthusiasm. "How about next Saturday?" Tiana suggested.

"That sounds perfect," Jake agreed. "If it snows, we'll go sledding at Northampton Park."

"And if there's no snow, we'll take a walk along the Erie Canal trail in Spencerport," Tiana added.

Ivy and Willow nodded in agreement, their faces lighting up at the plans.

"And we'll finish off with a late lunch in the village," Jake concluded, pleased with the arrangement.

The children's excitement was

unmistakable, their faces beaming with the prospect of another adventure together.

THE WEEK UNFOLDED with its usual array of life's demands. Tiana continued to contend with custody cases, including instances involving contentious custody battles and complex divorce settlements.

Meanwhile, the firehouse remained a hub of emergency responses, with challenges ranging from rescuing trapped animals to battling blazes in the local community.

Midweek, Jake and Ivy went to his parents' house for dinner. As they enjoyed their meal, Ivy couldn't contain her excitement.

"Nana, Papa, guess what?" Ivy started, her eyes twinkling. "I made a new friend, Willow! We're going sledding this Saturday."

Jake's parents looked at each other and smiled. "That sounds wonderful, Ivy," his mother said. "It's great to hear you're making new friends."

Jake added, "Willow's mom, Tiana, will be joining us too. It's nice to see Ivy so happy."

His father, with a curious glance, asked Jake, "And how have you been spending your time lately, son?"

Jake responded, "Well, between work

and spending time with Ivy, it's been quite busy. But we've been enjoying our time together, exploring new places, and just being there for each other."

The joy was evident on the grandparents' faces as they listened to Jake and Ivy. It was clear to them that their son and granddaughter had mended their relationship and were indeed thriving.

ON THAT SNOWY Saturday morning, Jake, Tiana, and their daughters met at Northampton Park. Excitement was in the air. Fresh snow covered every inch of the park.

"Look at all this snow! It's perfect for sledding!" said Ivy, her eyes wide with delight.

Willow, equally excited, nodded in agreement. "It's like a fairy tale!"

Tiana, with her radiant light brown skin and a cascade of beautiful, long curly hair that danced with the gentle breeze, brought a touch of warmth and elegance to the snowy landscape. She exuded a vibrant energy that seemed to harmonize with the glistening snowflakes.

Jake turned to her, smiling at the beautiful scene and her presence. "You look like you're part of this winter magic, Tiana. Ready to show us some sledding tricks?"

Tiana laughed, her hair catching the light of the winter sun. "I might just surprise you. But let's see who can sled the fastest. What do you say?"

Ivy and Willow's youthful enthusiasm was plain to see. With sleds in hand, they raced to the top of the snow-covered hill, their excited chatter rising like little puffs of warm breath in the chilly air.

The first slide down the snowy hill brought exhilaration and giggles, with their sleds gliding effortlessly on the powdery surface. Tiana's radiant smile and her infectious laughter were a testament to the sheer joy of the moment.

"This is amazing!" Tiana exclaimed, her laughter echoing across the hill.

Jake, equally thrilled, agreed. "It's like being a kid again! These sleds are perfect."

Each subsequent ride down the hill brought more excitement, with Ivy and Willow racing each other, their voices filled with glee. "Watch me go faster this time!" Ivy shouted, her sled picking up speed.

"I'm going to beat you!" Willow responded playfully, speeding down the hill alongside her. The sun cast a sparkling glow over the landscape. Jake and Tiana stood watching their daughters, clearly seeing the happiness in their rosy cheeks and sparkling eyes.

After a satisfying lunch, the group decided to pick up ice cream and apple pie to take back to Tiana's house and spend the rest of the day there. The girls had already set their hearts on watching the animated wonder of 'Moana.' It was a perfect choice for a day filled with adventure and the spirit of exploration. With their sweet treats in tow, they made their way to Tiana's home.

They all decided to watch the movie together. Nestled comfortably on the sofa, the four of them began enjoying the great combination of apple pie and ice cream. Their surroundings were filled with the warmth of friendship and the coziness of the moment.

When finally, this wonderful day came to an end, they exchanged heartfelt hugs, each eager to reconvene and create more cherished memories together in the near future.

Chapter 13

AMID THE BUSY and often chaotic moments of his life, Jake found himself experiencing a subtle yet profound shift in his thoughts. As he spent more time with Tiana and observed her in various settings, he couldn't help but notice the layers of depth in her character.

Her unwavering dedication to child advocacy was evident, and her passion for helping others shone through in every conversation they shared. Jake admired her resilience, the strength she exuded in her every word and action. Her radiant smile, her boundless empathy, and the beautiful way her curly hair framed her face all added to her magnetic allure.

Over time, the wall he had built around him after Emma died, began to crumble. As they shared stories from their past and confided in each other, a sense of connection blossomed within him.

Jake realized that Tiana was a remarkable woman in every sense. He thought of the quiet moments of camaraderie they shared, the way she made him laugh, the genuine interest she displayed, and how at ease he and Ivy felt around her and Willow.

While he initially admired her strength and resilience, he found himself drawn to her not just as a friend but as someone he was starting to see in a different light. He began to think about Tiana more often and the possibility of something deeper than friendship, a burgeoning sense of romance that was quietly taking root in his heart.

At the start of the week, he sent her a text, inviting her to join him for dinner. He made sure to emphasize it was a "dinner date." In response, she replied with a thumbs up and a cheerful smiley emoji.

On Wednesday evening, Jake arrived to pick up Tiana, and they headed to 'Bella Italia'. The restaurant's ambiance was warm and inviting, perfectly complementing the exquisite Italian cuisine they were about to enjoy.

As they savored each dish, Jake couldn't help but express his feelings. "Tiana, I have to say, I really enjoy spending time with you. These moments are something I look forward to," he said.

Tiana smiled, touched by his words. "I feel the same, Jake. It's not often you find someone you can be so open with."

Their conversation flowed effortlessly,

covering a range of topics. It was clear that they were comfortable in each other's presence, and even when they stumbled on differing viewpoints, they navigated the conversation with mutual respect and understanding. This newfound ease and compatibility only deepened their relationship as the evening unfolded.

Jake, feeling a sense of comfort, took a moment to add, "You are an incredible woman. Not just beautiful, but an amazing mom too. It's really admirable."

Tiana's eyes lit up with appreciation. "Thank you. That means a lot coming from you, especially seeing the kind of dedicated father you are."

Driven by curiosity, he asked, "I'm intrigued. How involved is Willow's father in your lives?"

Tiana paused for a moment, her expression thoughtful, and then replied, "He's not involved at all. In fact, she's adopted, and I've never actually met her biological father. It's quite a long and complicated story." Recognizing the sincerity of his interest, she continued, "I'm willing to share if you're interested and we have the time."

He nodded.

"In my early days of practicing law, I dedicated some of my time to pro bono work. One day, I received a phone call from a young woman—Jamie—whom I had previously represented in a drug-related case. I had managed to secure her community service and admission to a rehab program. Her call was filled with urgency. She needed to see me immediately. Without hesitation, I cleared my schedule for the upcoming hours and headed to the hospital, where she was.

"When I arrived, I was directed to the maternity ward. As I entered her room, I couldn't help but notice the red, swollen traces of tears on her face. She reached out her hand toward me, her words laden with emotion, she said, 'Thank you for coming. I know we haven't seen each other in a while, but I remember what an amazing woman you are from when you took my case a few years back. I couldn't think of anyone better to raise my daughter. I want you to raise her to be strong, intelligent, and caring, just like you.'

"Stunned and trying to make sense of her words, I asked her to explain. She proceeded to reveal to me, her tumultuous past, growing up in a well-to-do but emotionally distant family. Her struggles with drugs began in her teens as a way to cope with feelings of being unwanted and unloved. She confessed her inability to stay entirely clean during her pregnancy and revealed she had given birth to a baby girl the day before. Without knowing who the father was, she made a heartfelt plea for me to adopt her child.

"Overwhelmed by the unexpected request, I hesitated. I was flattered but pressed her as to why she or her family didn't want to raise the baby. Jamie told me she wanted her daughter to have love, support, and to grow up feeling wanted. Something she nor her parents were capable of doing. She said she believed I'd be a strong, loving role model.

"My emotions were running high as you can imagine. I told her I'd do it but only if she slept on it, and didn't change her mind by morning. With tears in my eyes, we shared a heartfelt hug before I headed for the door.

"But Jamie had one more request, the name. She wanted to name the baby Willow because when she was a little girl, she spent a lot of time with her grandmother. There was a beautiful willow tree in her backyard where she sought refuge beneath its strong branches––bending but never breaking. She wanted that for her daughter, a new life and the strength to withstand anything.

"The next day, I received a call from Jamie, confirming her decision to proceed with the adoption. It marked an unexpected, yet cherished and transformative change in my life."

As Tiana spoke, Jake gazed at her with admiration, struck by the selflessness she embodied.

"When Jamie asked me to become the mother of her daughter, it seemed like a subconscious echo of my own mother's love. My mother's unwavering devotion to me, regardless of the circumstances, was a testament to her belief that it was the right thing to do. In contrast, Jamie had chosen a different path, one characterized by selflessness and the pursuit of a safe and secure future for her child.

"In the realm of the profound bond between a mother and her child, the question arises: which path is truly right?"

"Tiana Williams," Jake said with awe in his voice, "you are an absolutely incredible woman." With those words, he leaned in and pressed a kiss to her lips.

Chapter 14

A S TIANA SPENT more time with Jake and Ivy, she couldn't help but notice the changes within herself. The sturdy emotional walls she had built over the years, meant to shield her from pain and disappointment, were slowly beginning to crumble in the warmth of their company.

One evening, during a reflective moment alone, Tiana mused to herself, "I never thought I'd let anyone in, not after everything. But there's something about Jake... his strength, his love for Ivy, it's... it's appealing."

In the following days, Tiana and Jake found reasons to call each other more frequently. During one such call, Tiana shared her thoughts.

"Jake, I've always admired how you are with Ivy, and the more time we spend together, the more I see the incredible man and father you are," she said, a hint of vulnerability in her voice.

Jake agreed, sounding happy. "Coming from you, that's incredibly meaningful to me. These moments we share, they're special. They feel different, in a good way—and—I miss you when we're apart."

Their conversations, once centered around their children and day-to-day life, began to delve into more personal reflections and shared dreams.

Tiana's realization of her growing romantic feelings for Jake was both surprising and heartwarming. It was a gentle shift in her emotions, a reminder that despite her past, life still had beautiful surprises in store.

One night, after a cozy dinner at Kaya's, they found themselves lingering outside. Jake reached out to gently take Tiana's hand. The contact sent a wave of unspoken emotions coursing through them both.

Their eyes met, and in that gaze, a world of feelings was exchanged.

"This feels right—special—magical," Jake whispered, his eyes reflecting the sincerity of his words.

Tiana, feeling the same rush of emotions, nodded in agreement, her heart racing. "It does," she responded softly, her eyes not leaving his.

The evening culminated in a passionate kiss as Jake dropped her off, leaving them both yearning for more. It was a kiss that spoke volumes. As he left, the lingering touch and longing looks were a silent promise of what was ahead.

THEY CONTINUED TO spend more time together, not only nurturing their growing romance but also creating precious memories with their daughters. Weekends often saw the two families exploring their city.

During one of their weekend outings, Ivy and Willow were buzzing with excitement as they prepared for their day out.

"Willow, guess what we're doing today?" Ivy exclaimed as they met up. "We're going to the museum to see the new art exhibition!"

Willow's face lit up. "Really? My favorite is the play area. It's so cool and so much fun."

They headed to the museum, Jake and Tiana talked while the girls continued their animated conversation. "I hope they have those cool history exhibits too," said Ivy. "Remember the last time, with the dinosaur bones?"

"Yeah, that was so cool!" Willow replied. "And what about the zoo later? I can't wait to see the monkeys!"

Their parents smiled, sharing a look of contentment at the girls' enthusiasm.

"Looks like we've got a full day ahead of us," Tiana said to Jake, who nodded in agreement.

THE DAY WAS filled with exploration and learning, from marveling at the art and history exhibits at the museum to the joy of watching animals at the zoo.

"I had such a fun day, Daddy," Ivy said. "So did I," parroted Willow.

In the evenings, Tiana and Jake often found joy in simple, cozy activities. Sometimes, they watched movies at home, with Ivy and Willow curled up on the sofa creating a warm atmosphere.

Jake often teased Tiana about her choice of pizza toppings, leading to playful banter. "You really like pineapple on your pizza?" he'd ask, feigning shock.

Tiana would respond with a laugh. "Absolutely! You don't know what you're missing!"

As their relationship deepened, moments of romance began to weave into their time together. Walking through the local fair, Jake would steal a quick kiss from Tiana. Their connection evolved from the platonic camaraderie of single parents sharing experiences to something more profound and intimate.

Tiana and Jake found themselves alone, enjoying quiet conversations. During one of these nights, Jake took Tiana's hand, his eyes reflecting his deepening feelings.

"Every moment with you feels deeply

intimate and perfect. I long for more and more with each passing day," he whispered.

In response, Tiana moved closer, her heart racing. The evening unfolded with enticing touches, and sensual kisses, followed by passion, as they explored their growing intimacy.

Their love story was blossoming beautifully. They were forging a path towards a shared future.

IN JUNE, TIANA had the pleasure of meeting Jake's parents, and it was a wonderful encounter. As they gathered in the living room, Jake's parents were thoroughly impressed by how at ease Jake, Tiana, and the girls were in each other's company.

"Tiana, we've heard so much about you." Jake's mother greeted her warmly, embracing her in a welcoming hug.

Tiana smiled, feeling a sense of belonging. "It's so nice to finally meet you both. Jake speaks so highly of you," she replied.

Over tea, Jake's father observed how well Ivy and Willow were playing together. "Look at them, just like sisters. It's wonderful to see Ivy so happy," he remarked.

"Yes, they get along amazingly

well," Tiana agreed, watching the girls with a fond smile. "They've become inseparable."

Jake, sitting beside Tiana, added, "It's not just the kids. Tiana has been an incredible part of our lives. She's been amazing with Ivy and... well, with me too."

His parents exchanged knowing smiles, clearly pleased. "We can see that, son. It's heartwarming to see you happy," his mother said.

Later, as Tiana helped in the kitchen, Jake's mother whispered to her, "You know, Emma was a wonderful woman, and she left a big gap in our lives. Seeing Jake and Ivy happy again with you... it feels right. Emma would have wanted that for them."

Tiana, touched by the sentiment, felt a deep sense of connection and acceptance, not just with Jake and Ivy, but with his entire family. The day marked not just an introduction but the weaving of Tiana and Willow, into the fabric of their lives, a blend of past and present, forming a hopeful and loving future.

As the weather warmed up, they decided to embark on a series of enjoyable adventures. Together, they planted a bountiful vegetable garden at Jake's house, bonding over the shared endeavor of nurturing new life. They also indulged in canoeing along Sandy Creek, reveling in the beauty of nature.

Their cultural side found expression in a trip to Geva Theatre to watch the enchanting show "Cinderella," a magical experience that captivated both the parents and the children. On other occasions, they explored the picturesque Erie Canal, enjoying long bike rides with scenic views as their backdrop.

The previously shattered heart of Jake and the deeply scarred soul of Tiana were now resolutely moving forward, wholeheartedly embracing the newfound glimmers of light that had begun to pierce the depths of their once-pervasive *'Abyss of Darkness.'*

Chapter 15

TIANA WAS PREPARING for her next appointment when she noticed the file on her desk was empty. As she wondered about the missing documents, her office door swung open, and her assistant ushered in a young woman.

"This is Ms. Taylor, your next appointment," her assistant announced.

Tiana's face lit up with recognition at seeing Jamie, but also noticed something different; a hint of illness in Jamie's appearance. "Hi, Jamie. You got married? Congratulations," she greeted her with a warm smile, her eyes showing a mix of happiness and concern

The somber look on Jamie's face quickly extinguished Tiana's cheerfulness. Her heart started to race as she sensed that Jamie was not here to exchange pleasantries.

Jamie spoke with resolve. "I want my baby back. I need her in my life right now. I know I've had my struggles, but I've changed. I can be a good mother to her."-

Tiana listened intently, her expression composed, but she could fell a chill run down her spine "I understand this must be incredibly difficult for you, Jamie. But we need to consider what's best for Willow. She's settled and thriving in a stable environment."

Jamie's hands trembled, and tears well up in her eyes; a mix of desperation and sadness.

Tiana continued, "Legally, the adoption is binding. Once the process is finalized, reversing it is extremely rare, especially if the child's well-being is not at risk."

Jamie, tears streaming down her face in desperation, pleads, "But I'm her real mother. Don't I have any rights at all?"

Tiana responded in a gentle yet firm tone, "As her mother now, I promise to give her all the love and care she needs. I can't imagine how hard this must be for you, but her stability is important."

As their conversation progressed, Jamie's realization that she had no legal rights to Willow became more apparent. The weight of this truth seemed to overwhelm her, and she broke down, a mix of sorrow and fear in her voice.

Through her tears, she revealed, "Tiana, my years of drug use have taken a toll on my body. The doctors... they've diagnosed me with liver disease. It's advanced, and they say it's terminal. I want to spend time with Willow––please. I want her to remember me."

Tiana listened, her expression filled with compassion. "Jamie, I had no idea. How long...?"

Jamie looked down, struggling with the words. "They've given me a few months, maybe a year at best. All those years of addiction... I never thought it would lead to this."

Tiana reaches out, offering a comforting hand. "I'm so sorry, Jamie. Is there anything I can do to help?"

Jamie's head shook faintly, her voice quivering with emotion. "Please, just... let me spend some time with Willow. I want to create happy memories, for both of us, for her to hold onto. I'm pleading with you––it means everything to me."

Tiana, after listening attentively to Jamie, nodded thoughtfully. "Jamie, I assure you, we'll arrange for you to spend time with Willow. But I need some time to process all this information and think about the best approach for her sake. How about we meet for lunch on Friday? We can discuss this further and plan out how to move forward."

Jamie, looking both relieved and grateful, stood up and hugged Tiana. "Thank you, Tiana. I'll see you on Friday, then," she said, her voice filled with gratitude.

THAT EVENING, AFTER putting the dishes away and tucking Willow into bed, Tiana sat beside her on the covers. She took a deep breath, knowing the conversation they were about to have was an important one.

"Willow, sweetie, I want to talk to you about something," Tiana began softly. "You know Jamie, who you've seen in pictures; your biological mom. She would like to spend some time with you."

Willow looked up, her young face a mix of curiosity and confusion. "My other mom? Why does she want to see me?"

Tiana chose her words carefully, wanting to be honest yet sensitive to her daughter's age. "Well, she cares about you a lot, and she wants to get to know you. It's a good thing, to have more people who love you."

"Will you be there too?" Willow asked, her small hand finding Tiana's.

"Of course, I'll be there," Tiana reassured her, squeezing her hand gently. "We can all meet together at the park. It'll be just like a regular playdate, but you'll get to meet Jamie and spend time with her."

Willow seemed to think about it for a minute. "Okay, Mommy. Can we play on the swings?"

Tiana smiled, relieved at her daughter's

response. "Yes, we can play on the swings. It'll be a nice time for all of us."

As Tiana kissed her goodnight, she felt a mix of apprehension and hope. She knew the road ahead might be complex, but she was determined to navigate it with love and openness for Willow's sake.

Chapter 16

TIANA SAT ACROSS from Jamie in the small café, the aroma of coffee mingling with the gravity of their conversation. Outside, the world rushed by, unaware of the delicate and crucial decisions being made within.

"Jamie, I've been thinking about how Willow can spend time with you," Tiana began, her tone gentle yet cautious. "I believe it's important for her to know you, but I think we should take it slow."

Jamie nodded, a look of understanding in her eyes. "I agree, and there's something I should tell you. I'm living with my parents now. I won't be alone with her. They've been a huge support."

Tiana felt a wave of relief. "That's good to hear, Jamie. It's important that Willow is in a safe and supportive environment."

Jamie played with her coffee cup, a nervous habit. "I was thinking, maybe Willow could visit us at my parents' house? You could come too, of course."

Tiana replied, "How about we start with shorter visits, with me present? We can have them at a nearby park, somewhere neutral. It would give Willow a chance to get to know you in a comfortable setting."

Jamie's face lit up with a hopeful smile. "That sounds perfect. I just want to make some happy memories with her. I want her to remember me."

"As do I," Tiana replied. "Let's plan for a weekend afternoon. We can have a picnic, make it fun for Willow."

The two women continued to discuss details, setting a date and time for their first meeting. It was a delicate balance of kindling a bond and protecting Willow's best interests.

As Tiana watched Jamie and Willow together, her heart was heavy with the knowledge of what lay ahead. Jamie's terminal illness cast a shadow over these meetings, turning each moment into something precious yet painfully finite. Tiana understood the importance of these encounters, not just for the joy they brought now, but for the memories they would leave for Willow.

The park visits became a series of bittersweet gatherings. Tiana observed as Jamie, with a quiet urgency, tried to compress a lifetime of love into each interaction with Willow. There was laughter and play, but also an underlying gravity as Jamie sought to leave a part of herself with her daughter.

In quiet moments, Tiana would reflect on the inevitable heartache that would come with Jamie's passing. *How will I explain this to Willow?* she often wondered. *How do I prepare her for the loss of a mother she's only just getting to know?*

Yet, amidst the sorrow, there was beauty in the way Jamie and Willow connected. Each smile, each hug, was a testament to the enduring nature of love, transcending even the most challenging circumstances.

Tiana was determined to make these days count, ensuring that Willow would have these memories to hold onto. It was a delicate balance of allowing joy in the present while bracing for the pain of the future.

Chapter 17

THE PAST FEW months had been an emotional rollercoaster for Tiana. The stress had worn her down, piece by piece, day by day. The relentless anxiety, the sleepless nights had taken a toll on her. Her life had been consumed by the worry for her daughter, leaving little room for anything else.

The stress seeped into every corner of her existence. Her once unbreakable spirit had been chipped away, her unwavering determination slowly eroded. The possibility of this being too much for Willow was an excruciating thought that had wrapped its icy fingers around her heart.

In the quiet of her bedroom, long after Willow had fallen asleep, Tiana lay awake, staring at the ceiling, lost in thought. The room was still, but her mind was anything but quiet.

"Did I make the right decision?" The weight of her choices pressing heavily on her. Bringing Jamie into Willow's life now, only for her to leave it so soon—was it fair to her daughter?

She thought about Willow, her bright, innocent eyes, and her joyful laughter. How would she cope with the loss of Jamie? Tiana feared that this might bring more pain than happiness in the long run. "Am I just setting her up for heartbreak?" she questioned herself, the doubt gnawing at her.

Tiana rolled over, her heart heavy with a guilt she couldn't shake. Here she was, wrestling with her decisions, while Jamie's remaining days were slipping away.

"How can I be so selfish?" she chastised herself. "Jamie deserves this time with Willow, no matter how short it may be." But even as she acknowledged this, her protective instincts as a mother battled with her empathy for Jamie. It was a torturous cycle of guilt and uncertainty.

Despite these restless thoughts, deep down, Tiana knew that love, even when fleeting, was a precious gift. She hoped that these memories with Jamie would someday be a source of comfort for Willow, not just a reminder of loss.

With a heavy heart, Tiana realized that there were no perfect answers, only the best choices she could make in an imperfect situation. As sleep finally claimed her, she whispered a silent hope for the strength to guide Willow through whatever lay ahead.

As THE DAYS passed and the reality of Jamie's passing away grew closer, Tiana found herself withdrawing from her usual circles, including Jake. Evenings that were once spent catching up with friends or sharing moments with Jake became solitary reflections or quiet nights in with Willow.

The gradual distancing from friends was not intentional, it was a protective mechanism, a way for Tiana to conserve her emotional resources for what she deemed most crucial—supporting Willow and preparing for the inevitable loss that would affect her deeply.

With Jake, it was even more complicated. She cherished the relationship they had and the support he had offered. Yet, as Jamie's condition worsened, Tiana felt an unspoken obligation to focus entirely on Willow and Jamie, to honor the time they had left. Her conversations with Jake became less frequent, and their time together dwindled. She recognized the hurt this may be causing him, but her mind was clouded with the pressing needs of the present.

Her life had narrowed down to this singular focus, she knew this period of her life required a different kind of strength and attention. It was a temporary retreat into a cocoon where she, Willow, and Jamie could navigate the complexities of their intertwined lives in the time they had left.

Chapter 18

AS SHE CONTINUED to distance herself from Jake, her feelings for him remained unresolved. She had found solace in his presence, a respite from the turmoil of her world, and the possibility of something more. Yet, the all-encompassing stress had made it impossible to explore these feelings. There was no room in her life for anyone but Willow.

One evening, Tiana made the heart-wrenching decision to let go of the one thing that had been both a distraction and a source of comfort during this turbulent time.

Tiana called Jake and asked to meet with him. They met under the shade of a large oak tree in the park. The atmosphere was thick with unspoken tension.

Jake approached Tiana with a slow, tender embrace, expressing the longing he'd been feeling. "Tiana, I've missed you and our times together so much," he said softly, his voice reflecting the depth of his feelings.

Tiana responded with a deep, sorrowful sigh. Her heart was heavy with the purpose of this encounter. She gently pulled back from Jake, her eyes haunted with sadness. Taking a deep breath, her voice trembled as she began to speak. "Jake, these past few months have been so hard. I'm struggling to hold myself together."

Jake's eyes were filled with concern and a deep understanding of her pain. He reached out, gently taking her hand. "Tiana, I see the strength it's taking for you to stand in this storm. I'm here for you, in whatever way you need. If you need space to breathe, I understand. But know this––you're not alone. I'm with you, every step of the way."

Tiana's eyes met Jake's, reflecting both gratitude and a deep sense of vulnerability. "Jake, having you here, means so much to me. but I'm terrified of not knowing how to manage all of the emotional turmoil. How will Willow react? How can I support her through Jamie's eventual loss? I realize this is not fair to you. My focus is so consumed by Willow and Jamie right now."

Her voice trembled as she continued, "But just knowing you're with me, even from a distance, it gives me a strength I didn't know I had. Yet, I feel a strong need to go through this next phase alone, even if it's only temporary. It's a journey I must embark on, for Willow's sake and for my own healing and understanding. As much as I want to have you by my side, I know in my heart this is something I need to do on my own."

Jake listened intently, his expression a blend of disappointment and understanding. He inhaled sharply before responding, his voice tinged with emotion.

"Tiana, hearing this isn't easy. I won't lie, it hurts, and I'm going to miss you and Willow more than I can say. But I respect your decision. I know this battle you're facing... it's deeply personal, and if stepping back for a short period of time is what you need to do for yourself and for Willow, then I support you. Just remember, no matter what, I'm here for you. When you're ready, I'll be waiting and hoping we can pick up where we left off."

His words were sincere, conveying his disappointment yet showing his utmost respect for her wishes.

With that, they exchanged a bittersweet hug, a longing kiss. A silent acknowledgment of the connection they had shared and the uncertain future they faced.

Chapter 19

THE MONTHS FOLLOWING Tiana's decision to pause her relationship with Jake were marked by a heavy silence. Tiana's life had shifted into a new routine, one that echoed with the absence of someone she had grown very close to.

Work remained a constant, but it had transformed into a refuge for Tiana, a place where she could channel her energy and dedication. She threw herself into her cases with even more intensity, determined to make a difference for children who needed her help. The courtroom became her second home, a place where she felt a sense of purpose, and where her legal expertise shone.

Yet, no matter how immersed she became in her work, there were moments when the silence in her life felt deafening. The absence of Jake, his laughter, and their shared moments left an ache in her heart. Willow missed Jake and Ivy too.

Tiana's friends, worried about her growing isolation, attempted to coax her into social activities, but she often declined, consumed by her maternal responsibilities.

Tiana's love for Willow had grown even deeper. She was determined to make every moment count with her daughter, to provide a stable and loving home. Their bond remained unwavering, the one bright light in Tiana's life.

THE SILENCE BETWEEN Tiana and Jake became a haunting reminder of the bond they had shared.

Tiana found herself alone with her thoughts. The silence around her echoed the void left by their unresolved relationship. Questions swirled in her mind, unrelenting and painful. *What if she had chosen differently? What could have been if circumstances were otherwise?* Each thought was a reflection of her inner turmoil, the struggle between her need for space and the undeniable bond she felt with Jake.

On many occasions, Tiana found herself instinctively reaching for her phone, her fingers hovering over Jake's contact, the desire to hear his voice was overwhelming. Yet, each time, she pulled back, reminding herself of the reasons behind her decision. Tiana's resolve to stay focused, to be the pillar of strength and love that Willow required, was her guiding force.

The absence of Jake remained a silent presence, a question mark in her heart that she wasn't yet ready to answer.

Chapter 20

IN THE MONTHS following Jamie's passing, Willow's life took on a somber tone, a stark contrast to the vibrant spirit of the little girl who once played without a care in the world.

During her time with Jamie, Willow had formed a bond with her biological mother—a connection that, though brief, had left an everlasting mark on her young heart. In their final visit, Jamie, though frail, mustered all her strength to speak to Willow from the heart.

"Willow, my sweet girl, remember that I love you so much, more than the stars in the sky and the fish in the sea. Remember that my love will always be with you, no matter where I am."

Willow, sitting beside her, looked up with innocent eyes, struggling to grasp the gravity of the moment. "Are you going to be with the stars, Mom?"

Jamie nodded gently, a tear rolling down her cheek. "Yes, my love. Someday, I'll be among the stars, watching over you. And even though I won't be here like this, my love will always surround you, like the air you breathe."

Willow clutched Jamie's hand, her young mind trying to make sense of it all. "But I don't want you to go, Mom. I'll miss you."

"I'll miss you too, my darling. But remember, every time you feel the warmth of the sun or see the beauty of a flower, that's my love reaching out to you." Jamie's voice quivered each word a whisper of her heart's deepest feelings. "And, Willow, be brave for me. Keep smiling, laughing, and playing. That's what will make me happiest," Jamie continued a mix of love and sadness in her eyes. Willow nodded, tears streaming down her face. "I'll try, Mom. I love you."

"I love you too, forever and always, my sweet girl," Jamie whispered, holding Willow's hand to her heart, a gesture of eternal connection.

IN THE WAKE of Jamie's death, Tiana found herself in the delicate role of helping her daughter navigate grief. "Mommy, why did Mom Jamie have to go?" Willow would often ask, her understanding of death still so naive.

"Sweetheart, sometimes people's bodies stop working, and they can't stay with us. But Jamie's love for you will never go away," Tiana would explain, holding Willow close, her own voice touched with sorrow.

Their conversations were a mix of reminiscing about the good times with Jamie and acknowledging the pain of her absence.

Tiana, though heartbroken herself, became a pillar of strength and comfort for Willow. She helped her daughter understand that it was okay to feel sad, to miss Jamie, but also important to remember the love and joy they shared.

It was a gradual process, one filled with difficult days and nights, but Tiana's unwavering support provided Willow with the resilience to face her loss and continue to grow with the loving memory of Jamie in her heart.

Chapter 21

FOR JAKE, THE days without Tiana felt incomplete. His heart longed for her, and his mind often drifted to the moments they had shared. Their conversations, laughter, and the way they had supported each other during difficult times lingered in his thoughts. There was an undeniable void in his life that only Tiana seemed to fill.

As he went about his daily routine, the echoes of their time together would suddenly resurface. A cup of coffee at a local café, the familiar park where they had taken the girls, even the sound of the wind through the trees—everything reminded him of Tiana. Her absence was like a silent ache that refused to fade.

Jake often found himself lost in thought, reflecting on his decision to give Tiana space. "She's going through so much right now," he reminded himself, trying to justify his absence. "She needs this time to focus on Willow and deal with Jamie's passing."

Yet, in the quiet of the night, Jake

couldn't help but question his decision. "Am I doing the right thing by staying away? Maybe she needs me now, more than ever." His heart ached with the thought that he might be failing her when she needed him the most.

As he lay in bed, staring at the ceiling, he remembered Tiana's smile, her strength, and the way she faced challenges head-on. "She's incredible. But even the strongest people need support," he murmured to himself. The longing to reach out, to be there for her, tugged at him relentlessly.

Despite his commitment to give her the time she needed, Jake grappled with a deep sense of missing her and a desire to be by her side. It was a conflict between respecting her need for space and his instinct to be there for her.

Each day that passed without contact was a struggle, a balance between his respect for her wishes and the growing concern that maybe, just maybe, his support was what she needed to navigate through the turmoil.

MEANWHILE, TIANA FACED a similar struggle. Her mind often strayed to Jake. His carefree chuckles, the way he cared for Ivy, and the strength of the bond they'd built—it had all left an indelible mark on her heart.

One evening, Willow, with her innocent curiosity, asked, "Mommy, when will we see Jake and Ivy again? I miss them."

Tiana paused for a moment, her heart tightening. She had expected this question to come eventually, but the answer was far from simple.

She replied softly, "Sweetie, I'm not sure. We've had some changes in our lives, and we might not see them for a while."

Willow's face showed her disappointment, and Tiana felt a pang of sorrow. She missed Jake and knew that Willow did too.

AS THE WEEKS passed, she contemplated reaching out to Jake, her mind wrestling with the uncertainty of his reaction after their separation.

Should I call? she wondered aloud one evening, gazing at the phone. *But what if he resents me for pausing things between us?What if he's moved on?* The thought of rekindling their relationship brought both hope and anxiety.

She missed him, more than she had anticipated. Every little thing seemed to remind her of Jake, a joke he would have appreciated, a situation he would have had advice for. Her heart ached for the connection they had shared, a bond that seemed to grow stronger in his absence.

"But I was the one who paused things," Tiana reminded herself, sighing. "I can't just expect him to be waiting. And what about Willow? I need to think about what's best for her too."

Despite these reservations, Tiana couldn't shake off the feeling that what she and Jake had was special. It was more than just a fleeting romance; it was a deep bond that had brought joy and comfort to both their lives and the girls. She found herself at a crossroads, torn between the desire to reach out and the apprehension of facing rejection.

Chapter 22

HALLOWEEN WAS JUST around the corner, and Tiana decided to make a trip to Kelli's farm with Willow to pick out some pumpkins. It had been an annual tradition for them. As they strolled through the pumpkin patch, Willow's eyes sparkled with excitement. She carefully examined each pumpkin, trying to find the perfect one to carve into a spooky jack-o'-lantern.

Tiana watched her daughter with a mixture of pride and nostalgia. Willow was growing up so fast, and these moments together were becoming even more precious.

Last year, around the same time, they had run into Jake and Ivy at the farm. Tiana remembered vividly how Jake's eyes had lit up as he saw her, and how the kids had played together in the sprawling pumpkin patch.

But this year was different. As Tiana glanced around, she didn't spot Jake or Ivy anywhere. Their absence was felt, and Tiana couldn't help but wonder what they were up to. Were they busy moving forward in their lives?

Despite their absence, Tiana and Willow found joy in the simple act of picking pumpkins. They carefully selected several different sizes and shapes. It was a beautiful, sunny day, and the farm was bustling with families and children in costumes.

After gathering their pumpkin treasures, they treated themselves to warm apple cider and freshly made donuts, savoring the delicious flavors of the season.

As they made their way back home, Willow excitedly chattered about the creative designs she wanted to carve into her pumpkins. Tiana smiled, her heart warmed by the love she felt for her daughter.

A FEW WEEKS before Christmas, Jake had several important visits scheduled at the local elementary school. He was invited to educate children about fire safety, particularly during the holiday season when homes were filled with lights, decorations, and Christmas trees.

During one of the visits, Jake arrived at the school carrying his full firefighting gear, including his helmet and jacket as part of show and tell. His presence generated a sense of excitement and curiosity among the students.

The classroom was adorned with festive decorations, and a beautifully decorated Christmas tree stood in one corner, capturing the essence of the season. Jake began by introducing himself and his role as a firefighter, explaining how important it was to stay safe during the holiday season. He noticed Willow in the room and winked at her.

He spoke about the potential fire hazards that could arise from Christmas lights, candles, and the Christmas tree itself. As he concluded his presentation, Jake opened the floor for questions, and Willow's hand shot up immediately.

"Have you ever put out a fire in someone's Christmas tree?"

Jake chuckled. "Well, I've seen some close calls."

Following the presentation, the students were given the opportunity to explore the firetruck parked just outside the school. As the children were being guided to the parking lot, Jake approached Willow.

"I've missed you and your mommy, Willow."

She beamed with excitement. "I miss you and Ivy too. We should have a movie night at our house, just like we used to. We can watch a movie, and eat some ice cream and popcorn. It would be so much fun! I'll tell Mommy." She gave Jake a hug, her youthful enthusiasm shining through, and then rejoined her fellow students.

THAT EVENING, WILLOW excitedly burst through the door, her eyes shining. She greeted her mother with a warm hug.

"Mom, guess what? I saw Jake today at school, and he told us all about how to stay safe with our Christmas tree. He's a real superhero! We decided we have to have movie night again. This weekend, okay? Pleeeaseeee?"

Tiana smiled. If she'd been waiting for the right time to reconnect with Jake, fate just handed it to her.

"Not this weekend but soon." Now she just had to find the courage to call him.

Chapter 23

JAKE AND IVY celebrated Christmas Eve with his parents. The house was adorned with decorations and the welcoming aroma of holiday dishes cooking in the kitchen.

The windows were illuminated with twinkling lights, and a beautifully decorated Christmas tree stood in the living room, glistening with ornaments and tinsel. Together, they enjoyed a festive dinner that included all their favorite holiday dishes.

On Christmas morning, Ivy and Jake woke up to the magic of the day in their own home, surrounded by the glow of holiday lights. Together, they baked cinnamon rolls and made hot chocolate before heading toward the Christmas tree where they exchanged gifts.

Ivy's eyes sparkled with excitement as she carefully unwrapped her presents from Jake. Following the gift-giving, they lounged around watching some of their favorite Christmas movies.

On New Year's Eve, a crisp winter's day, Jake decided to take Ivy ice skating at Manhattan Square Park. There was an undeniable longing in his heart, a hope that he might run into Tiana. As they laced up their skates and prepared to glide onto the glistening ice, destiny granted his wish. There, donned in a striking red scarf and hat, stood Tiana, Willow at her side. Tiana's long, bouncy curls danced in the wind, impossible to miss.

Jake's heart raced as he watched Willow and Ivy spot each other and dash toward an enthusiastic reunion. Tiana stepped gracefully off the ice and joined Jake, a warm smile on her face, as the past and present collided in the heart of a winter haven.

"Happy New Year. Fancy seeing you here," Jake remarked with a grin, the cool air punctuating his words.

Tiana chuckled, her breath forming delicate wisps in the winter night. "Happy New Year. You know I always bring Willow here for New Year's Eve, Mr. Donovan."

Jake couldn't help but join in her laughter. "Guilty as charged, Miss Williams," he admitted playfully, a shared amusement wrapping them in a moment of unspoken rapport between them.

They skated, stopped for cookies and cocoa, and then watched the fireworks. The kaleidoscope above painted a shimmering backdrop to their conversation. The sight of her under the burst of colorful lights was a vision that held him captivated.

He couldn't help but notice how she hadn't changed, how that warmth, that undeniable spark in her eyes, was still there, as radiant as ever.

In the midst of the joyful New Year's celebration, Jake took a step closer. He let his voice drop to a hushed whisper, an intimate confession meant only for her ears.

"Tiana," he began, his words laced with vulnerability and sincerity, "I've missed you...and I want you!" It was a truth he had carried with him for far too long, and he couldn't hold it in any longer. "I've missed both you and Willow. Life took us on separate paths, but it never quite felt complete without the two of you ."

Tiana met his gaze, her eyes reflecting the shimmering display of fireworks overhead. In that moment, the world around them seemed to fade, replaced by an intense sense of anticipation. His words hung in the air, heavy with the weight of the past year, filled with shared moments, and laden with the unspoken longing that had lingered between them.

"Jake," she began, her voice a delicate

mix of emotion, "I've missed you more than I can say."

Tiana leaned closer, closing the distance between them, and planted a kiss on Jake's lips. As she pulled away, she whispered, "I-I don't know. I'm scared, Jake."

However, before she could continue, he cut her off with a long, intense kiss, filled with passion that left her breathless.

"Tiana, you've emerged from the abyss of life's trials and tribulations as a strong, intelligent, beautiful, and caring woman. You're a remarkable mother. But I also see the walls you've built around you to protect yourself from getting hurt." He paused, inhaling deeply to gather his composure. "When we construct walls around ourselves to avoid getting hurt, we inadvertently stop truly living. I know, because I shut the world out when Emma died. Love is about embracing the full spectrum of emotions, both joy and pain. It's in these experiences, in the breadth of feeling, that we find the essence of love. That's what it's all about, not just the happiness, but the entire journey of the heart."

Jake gathered his resolve, his declaration unwavering, frustration simmered beneath his words.

"I love you," he said exasperated, his determination apparent. "I'm willing to wait as long as it takes for those barriers to crumble. I've journeyed through the darkest of times and emerged stronger. Missing you, wanting to be with you, that's my reality! I know you feel the same. So, it's time to cast aside those blinders, tear down those walls that stand between us. Now you know how I feel and where to find me."

He sealed his impassioned tirade with another fiery kiss, rendering her breathless and speechless this time. He turned and walked toward Willow and wished her a Happy New Year and gave her a hug. He took Ivy's hand and left, not looking back.

TIANA STOOD THERE, stunned by the whirlwind of emotions and newfound realizations. Her heart raced, but it wasn't fear that gripped her now, it was something entirely different. A sense of fullness and completeness like she had never experienced before.

Was she in love with Jake too? The question lingered, like a promise awaiting an answer, in the midst of fireworks and the dawn of a new year.

Chapter 24

THE NEW YEAR had begun with a passionate exchange and profound confessions, but as January unfolded, silence settled once more between Jake and Tiana.

Jake found himself replaying that last kiss and the stunned look on Tiana's face in the solitude of his home. Ivy occasionally mentioned Tiana and Willow, curious about her whereabouts. The answer always escaped him, as he grappled with the unfamiliar territory of patience. He had declared his love for Tiana and his willingness to wait, but waiting was more challenging than he had anticipated.

MEANWHILE, TIANA'S THOUGHTS wandered to Jake. The boldness of their New Year's Eve encounter still resonated with her. She could sense the fullness he had brought to her life, like a missing puzzle piece falling into place. The thought of Jake loving her, despite her carefully constructed walls, was both terrifying and intoxicating. The more she contemplated it, the clearer it became that she, too, wanted more. The challenge now was not just to tear down those walls but to navigate the uncertain terrain beyond them.

Despite the silence, the month of January was filled with a shared longing and a sense of unfinished business that hung in the air like a tantalizing promise, but taking that next step would be a journey they'd have to undertake with care and patience.

IT WAS A biting cold February day when Jake, reluctantly found himself in court once again. A subpoena had summoned him to testify regarding an accident he had witnessed while on duty. The memory of that dreadful day was still vivid, the events replaying in his mind as he prepared to relive them on the stand. The incident had been a catastrophic building collapse in the heart of the city.

As he left the courtroom after his testimony, he found himself in the chaos of the lobby of the courthouse, his heart heavy, he sat for a few minutes to clear his head. The images he had relived in the courtroom so vivid.

He got up as Tiana entered the lobby. Her presence seemed to breathe peacefulness into the courthouse surroundings.

They took steps toward each other, and their gaze intensified. They stood inches apart. In that silent moment, a world of emotions passed between them. It was a look that spoke of longing, of unfinished conversations, and of feelings left unspoken.

Just as Jake began to step away, Tiana reached out and grabbed his hand, her eyes locking onto his.

In a voice barely above a whisper, she confessed the same truth he had boldly proclaimed a month earlier.

"I love you too, Jake," she said, and with those words, their lips met in a kiss that held the entirety of their affection. It lingered, a testament to the depth of their feelings until the applause of onlookers broke the trance echoing through the courthouse lobby.

With their hands still intertwined, Jake and Tiana shared a look of joy, gratitude, and the realization that they had found their way back to each other. Amidst the cheers of onlookers who had witnessed their reunion, Jake and Tiana stood together, ready to embark on the next chapter of their journey.

Epilogue

TIANA HAD ALWAYS been a believer in love, but nothing could have prepared her for the moment when love truly took hold of her life, and made the choice to spend forever with the incredible man who had found his way back to her.

About a year after Jake and Tiana reconnected, he proposed in the most heartfelt and romantic way.

They were on a hiking trip in the mountains, surrounded by the serenity of nature and a breathtaking view. Jake got down on one knee and asked Tiana to marry him. The ring he held out, a symbol of his love and their future together, glistened in the sunlight. With tears of joy in her eyes, she said yes. The moment was magical, and it marked the beginning of yet another beautiful chapter in their life.

The journey from engagement to marriage was a whirlwind of joy, love, and planning. Jake and Tiana decided that the land where they would eventually build their dream house was the perfect place for their wedding. It was their sanctuary, their shared dream, a symbol of their love and the life they were creating together.

The day of Tiana and Jake's wedding was nothing short of magical. They chose to keep it simple, surrounded by the natural beauty of the land. Their friends and family gathered under a clear, sunny sky, with the vibrant colors of nature as their backdrop. Ivy and Willow, dressed in matching flower girl dresses, spread petals along the aisle as Tiana walked toward Jake.

The ceremony was a beautiful fusion of their love, shared promises, and the cheers and blessings of their loved ones. They exchanged vows, sealing them with a kiss. The world seemed to stand still, and in that moment, it was just Jake and Tiana, promising to be together forever.

Their simple and intimate reception featured a heartfelt speech from Jake and a special dance between Ivy, Willow, and their father. They celebrated with delicious food and laughter, surrounded by the warmth of their family and friends. Their wedding day was a true reflection of the two of them, filled with love, simplicity, and the promise of a beautiful future together.

Tiana Williams'

Diary

3 years later

DEAR DIARY,
It's incredible to think that thirty-six months have passed since Jake and I found our way back to each other and began building a life filled with love, growth, and shared dreams. These past three years have been nothing short of amazing, and they continue to unfold with new stories, experiences, and the bond that has deepened with each passing day.

The early months were a whirlwind of discovering one another again, of unearthing the people we had become during our time apart. The walls I had built around me started to crumble under Jake's gentle persistence, and his unwavering support allowed me to trust again. Our connection grew, not just in our love for each other but in our love for our two beautiful girls.

There were certainly bumps along the way, of course. But with Jake's support and understanding, we've managed *to navigate through the rough waters, reminding ourselves of the love that brought us together in the first place.*

Our growing love is paralleled by the growth of our two incredible daughters. Willow and Ivy have become the best of friends, and seeing their bond grow brings me immense joy. They've helped each other heal in ways I could never have imagined. Willow has discovered her calling in the art of dance, specifically ballet. It's been a joy to watch her grace the stage with her every move, the embodiment of elegance and poise. Ivy, on the other hand, has wholeheartedly embraced soccer. Not only has she become a skilled player, but her involvement in the sport has also allowed her to make new friends, teaching her the value of teamwork and camaraderie. Watching our girls follow their passions and thrive has been a source of immense pride and joy.

In addition to our two wonderful daughters, our family has grown by one more member—a furry, three-legged friend we adopted, an Australian Shepherd. Phoenix's journey mirrored our own in some ways, as he had also overcome adversity. His resilience and spirit shone through, even though one of his legs had to be amputated due to mistreatment by previous owners.

Since adopting him, Phoenix has brought an extra layer of warmth and love to our home. His boundless energy and playful spirit have endeared him to all of us, and his presence has added a unique and heartwarming dimension to our family dynamic. We are grateful for his unwavering loyalty and the lessons of resilience and hope he teaches us every day.

One significant project that Jake and I have embarked on is building our dream house. The idyllic piece of land we found, with several acres of space surrounded by towering trees, feels like something out of a fairy tale. Our new home is not just a house but a sanctuary where love and dreams take shape. It's a testament to our shared commitment and a place where we create memories together with our girls, day by day.

As I sit here writing this entry, I'm reminded once again that life's journey is not always straightforward. Some questions may never be fully answered, but it's the love and strength we have in the present that truly matters. With Jake, Ivy, Willow, and Phoenix by my side, I'm ready to embrace the future, whatever it may bring.

Our days are filled with laughter, the delightful sounds of our children's footsteps, and the simplicity of shared moments. *Our love, which rekindled after an* **abyss of darkness***, remains a strong and comforting presence in our lives. It's the force that propels us forward, allowing us to face every challenge with strength and unity.*

I can't help but smile at the thought of the love story we've lived and the incredible journey we're on. I'm grateful for every moment, and I'm eager to see where our love will lead us next.

The End

About the Author

Marcelina Nóbrega Courtney

I cherish my family.
Growing up with ten siblings was a mix of fun and chaos.
I find peace in silence and come alive with the rhythm of music.
While I have a fondness for unique shoes, I'm most comfortable barefoot.
I love walking in the rain; it feels rejuvinating to me.
I'm on a journey towards embracing body positivity.
I live life with an attitude of gratitude.
Writing is a hobby and a passion for me; not a job.
May my stories find a special place in your heart.

Made in the USA
Middletown, DE
03 January 2024

46928563R00080